PHANTOM

Book by
ARTHUR KOPIT

Music and Lyrics by
MAURY YESTON

Based on the novel "The Phantom of the Opera"
by GASTON LEROUX

S A M U E L   F R E N C H ,   I N C .
45 WEST 25TH STREET   NEW YORK 10010
7623 SUNSET BOULEVARD   HOLLYWOOD 90046
LONDON   *TORONTO*

Amateurs wishing to arrange for the production of PHANTOM must make application to SAMUEL FRENCH, INC., at 45 West 25th Street, New York, NY 10010, giving the following particulars:

(1) The name of the town and theatre or hall of the proposed production.

(2) The maximum seating capacity of the theatre or hall.

(3) Scale of ticket prices.

(4) The number of performances intended and the dates thereof.

(5) Indicate whether you will use an orchestration or simply a piano.

Upon receipt of these particulars SAMUEL FRENCH, INC., will quote terms and availability.

Stock royalty quoted on application to SAMUEL FRENCH, INC., 45 West 25th Street, New York, NY 10010.

For all other rights than those stipulated above, apply to Flora Roberts, Inc., 157 West 57th Street, New York, NY 10019 and The Tantleff Office, 375 Greenwich St., Ste. 700, New York, NY 10013.

An orchestration consisting of:

Piano/conductor's score	Horns I & II
Keyboards	Trombone
Reed I (Flute, Piccolo, Alto flute)	Violins I & II
Reed II (Oboe, English horn)	Cellos I & II
Reed III (Clarinet)	Violas
Reed IV (Flute, Clarinet, Bass clarinet)	Bass
Reed V (Bassoon)	Trumpets I & II

Percussion (Bass drum [concert - 36"], Bells [orchestra], Bell tree, Chimes, Drum set, Finger cymbals, Glockenspiel, Gong, Ratchet, Suspended cymbal, Tam-tam [large - 30"] Tympani [2 - 26" and 29"], Triangle, Wood block Xylophone) - 2 books

Harp

25 chorus books

will be loaned two months prior to the production ONLY on receipt of the royalty quoted for all performances, the rental fee and a refundable deposit. The deposit will be refunded on the safe return to SAMUEL FRENCH, INC. of all materials loaned for the production.

Printed in the U.S.A.
ISBN 0 573 69341 2

IMPORTANT BILLING AND CREDIT REQUIREMENTS

The names of Arthur Kopit and Maury Yeston shall receive billing in any and all advertising and publicity issued in connection with the licensing, leasing and renting of the Work for stock and amateur production hereunder. Their billing shall appear in, but not be limited to all theatre programs, houseboards, billboards, marquees, displays, posters, throwaways, circulars, announcements, and advertisements (except ABC ads), and whenever and wherever the title of the Work appears and shall be on separate lines immediately following the title of the Work as indicated below. The Owners' names shall be equal in size, type and prominence and in size of type at least Fifty Percent (50%) of the largest letter of the title type and no names shall be equal in size of type to those of Arthur Kopit and Maury Yeston. No credits shall be larger than the credits afforded the Owners except the title and the names of stars appearing above the title and no names shall be equal to that of Arthur Kopit and Maury Yeston. The billing and credits shall be in the following form:

(Name of Producer)
presents

PHANTOM

Book by Arthur Kopit
Music and Lyrics by Maury Yeston
Based on the novel "The Phantom of the Opera" by Gaston Leroux

The following credit shall appear on the title page of all programs and on all billboards, posters and other paid advertising in which the producers, creative and technical staff receive credit, and shall not be less than Fifty Percent (50%) of the credit accorded the scenic designer of such production:

"Originally Produced in the United States at Theatre Under the Stars, Houston, Texas
Originally directed by Charles Abbott"

CHARACTERS

THE PHANTOM	The Opera Ghost, also known as Erik
CHRISTINE DAEÉ	the Phantom's protege
THE COUNT DE CHANDON (PHILIPPE)	in love with Christine
GERARD CARRIERE	former manager of the Opera House
CHOLET	new manager of the Opera House
CARLOTTA	the new diva; Cholet's wife
JEAN-CLAUDE	the stage manager
INSPECTOR LEDOUX	chief of the Paris police

Various members of the opera company, police, the Phantom's Acolytes

ACT I

[Music Cue #1: OVERTURE]

Curtain up on the magnificent Avenue de l'Opera, Paris, turn of the century. It is late afternoon. In the distance, the Opera House looms against the sky.

On the street is a small, make-shift flea market with VENDORS selling bread, balloons, flowers, an ARTIST with an easel and brushes, a JUGGLER and a marionette show. A very festive place.

Enter CHRISTINE DAEÉ a girl in her early twenties and beautiful in an innocent, angelic way. Her clothes suggest she's a country girl. But though simple, they are lovely.

SHE carries a case and a small portable stand with folding legs.

[Music Cue #2: MELODIE DE PARIS]

CHRISTINE.
LA LA LA LA LA LA LA
LA LA LA LA LA LA LA
LA LA LA LA LA LA LA
LA …
   ONE OF THE CROWD. Bonjour, mademoiselle!
   CHRISTINE. Bonjour!
LA LA LA LA LA LA LA
LA LA LA LA LA LA LA
LA LA LA LA LA LA LA
LA …

(The CROWD starts inching towards her, curious to find out who she is and what she's carrying.)

5

SECOND MEMBER OF CROWD. Who is she?
THIRD MEMBER OF CROWD. Never seen her before. (*To yet another member of crowd.*) Have you?

(This other PERSON shakes head—no one knows who she is.)

CHRISTINE.
LA LA LA LA LA LA LA
LA LA LA LA LA LA LA
LA LA LA LA LA LA LA
LA ...

(As she sings, CHRISTINE starts to set up her stand. Then SHE opens the case she's brought. The CROWD's curiosity is growing; THEY move in.)

FOURTH MEMBER OF CROWD. What's she selling?

(The OTHERS shake their heads. By now, a crowd has gathered around her.)

CHRISTINE.
LA LA LA LA LA LA LA
LA LA LA LA LA LA LA
LA LA LA LA LA LA LA
LA ...
FIFTH MEMBER OF CROWD. (*To Christine.*) What have you got there for us, mademoiselle?
CHRISTINE. (*Taking out sheets of paper.*) A new song. For *sale!* Just published! All about Paris!

(EVERYONE seems excited by this.)

VARIOUS PEOPLE. Ahhh! Paris!

(CHRISTINE hands out sheet music. SHE continues to sing.)

CHRISTINE. *(Sings.)*
MELODY MELODY MELODY MELODY
SUNG SO MELODIOUSLY
MELODY MELODY
MY KIND OF MELODY
GENTLE AND FLOWING AND FREE ...

SOARING ABOVE EVERY ROOFTOP
WHISPERING UNDER EACH TREE
MELODY MELODY
MY MELODIE DE PARIS ("pa-ree") ...
    ONE OF THE CROWD. Let me see a copy of that.
    ANOTHER PERSON. I'll have one, too.
    CHRISTINE.
PARIS IS THE RAIN
PARIS IS THE PAIN OF A LOVER'S GOODBYE
IT'S THE STARE
WHEN YOUR EYE MEETS A STRANGER
EVER DANGEROUS ...
    VARIOUS PEOPLE/CHRISTINE. *(As THEY read the music.)*
PARIS IS THE SUN ...
    CHRISTINE. That's right!
PARIS, IF THERE'S ONE PERFECT PLACE
I MUST BE
IT CAN ONLY BE HERE IN PARIS!

(The handsome COUNT DE CHANDON, heir to the champagne fortune, enters with two beautiful WOMEN and a SERVANT.)

ENSEMBLE.
MELODY MELODY MELODY MELODY
SUNG SO MELODIOUSLY

VARIOUS PEOPLE. Look! It's the Count de Chandon! / The Count de Chandon! / Bonjour, Monsieur le Count!
ENSEMBLE.
MELODY MELODY
MY KIND OF MELODY
GENTLE AND FLOWING AND FREE ...
CHRISTINE.
SOARING ABOVE EVERY ROOFTOP
WHISPERING UNDER EACH TREE
ENSEMBLE.
MELODY MELODY
MY MELODIE DE PARIS

(Some of the WOMEN in the crowd preen as the COUNT passes through. CHRISTINE remains oblivious of the Count's arrival.
The COUNT hears CHRISTINE singing; her voice and beauty draw him towards her.
The WOMEN he's with are not pleased by this.)

BOTH WOMEN. *(With annoyance, together.)* Philippe!

(HE waves to them to be patient. THEY throw up their arms in typical French exasperation. THEY sulk.
The COUNT approaches Christine. Though HE pretends he's interested in buying her music, it's clear that HE is interested in her.
By now, the word that the Count de Chandon is here has spread, and PEOPLE make way for him as HE approaches Christine.)

THE COUNT. Mademoiselle, forgive this intrusion. What is your name?
CHRISTINE. Christine Daeé.

THE COUNT. Christine Daeé, I am Philippe de Chandon, a connoisseur of music, and beauty.

A CUSTOMER. (*To Christine.*) Mademoiselle?

THE COUNT. You waste your time selling songs.

CHRISTINE. (*Shocked.*) ... What?

THE COUNT. It's true. It's not fair. *All* Paris should hear your voice. (*Softly, seductively.*) That is how good you are. (*Matter-of-fact.*) Have you ever considered a career in the opera?

CHRISTINE. (*Stares at him, stunned.*) ... In the *opera*?

THE COUNT. I can see you have. You'll of course need lessons. A fine, natural voice is not nearly enough, as I'm sure you know. (*Drawing out a business card and writing on it as he talks.*) Here is my card. I am one of the opera's principal patrons. (*HE smiles and hands her his card.*) Present this to Gerard Carriere, the company manager, and he'll take care of you. I'd take you there myself but, alas, business calls me away.

BOTH OF THE COUNT'S WOMEN. (*Together, angrily.*) Philippe!

THE COUNT. Yes, yes! I'm coming! (*To Christine.*) My business associates. (*HE takes CHRISTINE's hand and kisses it.*) Christine! A tout a l'heure.

(*HE goes to the two ladies and THEY exit.
CHRISTINE, dazzled, stares after him, then at the card in her hand.*)

MEMBER OF THE CROWD. *The Count de Chandon*!

SECOND MEMBER OF THE CROWD. The champagne king!

CHRISTINE. (*Clutching the card to her bosom, stares at the Opera House.*) Me ... at the Paris Opera! (*SHE sings.*)

PARIS IS A FOOL
PARIS IS THE BOULANGERIE ON THE SQUARE
IT'S THE AIR OVER FIELDS CALLED "ELYSIAN"
AH, PARISIAN AIR!

PARIS IS L'AMOUR
PARIS, COMME TOUJOURS
IF THERE'S ONE PLACE FOR ME
IT IS ONLY ICI A PARIS!
   ENSEMBLE.
MELODY MELODY MELODY MELODY
SUNG SO MELODIOUSLY
MELODY MELODY
MY KIND OF MELODY
GENTLE AND FLOWING AND FREE

SOARING ABOVE EVERY ROOFTOP
WHISPERING UNDER EACH TREE
MELODY MELODY
MY MELODIE DE PA ...
MELODY MELODY
MY ME-LODIE DE PA-RIE ...

(ALL begin to exit except CHRISTINE, who turns and stares toward the Opera House.)

DE PARIS ...
DE PARIS ...

(The MUSIC darkens. The LIGHTS fade. We hear TWO VOICES; a woman's and a man's.)

   CARLOTTA. (*Imperiously.*) Well, what are you waiting for?
   BUQUET. (*Scared.*) One of the stage hands said I shouldn't go down here.

CARLOTTA. Monsieur Buquet, who are you working for, the stage hands or me?

BUQUET. You, Madame Carlotta.

CARLOTTA. Then GET GOING!

BUQUET. (*Scared.*)Yes, Madame Carlotta.

(We scrim through to a great stone staircase under the stage of the Opera House. JOSEPH BUQUET, in workman's clothes and holding a lantern, descends the stairs in terror.
As HE descends, we hear ...)

CARLOTTA. I want an inventory of everything you can find down there! Old costumes, old sets ... I want to know exactly what it is my husband and I are inheriting.

(We hear the SOUND of a heavy metal door leading to the cellar stairs shutting with a clang.)

BUQUET. (*To himself, scared.*) ... Yes, Madame Carlotta ...

(As BUQUET descends in terror, the lower domain begins to come into view. It's a catacomb of shadows and gloom. LIGHTS fade on Buquet and come up on...
THE PHANTOM'S DOMAIN, a realm of gloom and mist. We can hear MEN'S VOICES, singing. They are the Phantom's ACOLYTES. THEY emerge from the shadows. They're a wretched-looking group, dressed in rags. THEIR faces are never fully visible. Along with the acolytes, we can see an armoire filled with the Phantom's masks. These masks are each on a stand and are extraordinary and of varying expressions. Many are jeweled.)

[Music Cue #2A: PHANTOM ENTRANCE]

ACOLYTES.
AHHHHHHH …
AHHHHHHH …
AHHHHHHH …

(The PHANTOM appears out of the darkness.
HE is dressed elegantly, as if for a First Night. HE
begins to try on various masks. As he does, HE
sings.)

THE PHANTOM.
PARIS IS A TOMB. PARIS IS A ROOM WITH FOUR
  WALLS
AND NO LIGHT …
PARIS IS THE NIGHT!
ACOLYTES. *(Sing.)*
AHHHHHHH …
AHHHHHHH …
AHHHHHHH …

(Suddenly, JOSEPH BUQUET appears on a staircase.
THE PHANTOM, sensing an intrusion, looks up,
mask in his hand but none on his face. HIS back is to
the audience. We do not see his face.
THE PHANTOM sees Buquet at the moment BUQUET
sees him. BUQUET cries out in horror. THE
PHANTOM puts his mask on and points at Buquet.
THE ACOLYTES move in on BUQUET. BUQUET
screams and LIGHTS go to BLACK.
LIGHTS COME UP on the main level above, backstage,
where members of the COMPANY are getting into
make-up and costume for the evening's performance,
as well as to a lounge where LADIES of Parisian
Society are doing last minute primping.)

[Music Cue #3: DRESSING FOR THE NIGHT]

ACTORS. (*Sing.*)
DRESSING FOR THE NIGHT,
FOR THE BALL, FOR THE DANCE
DRESSING FOR THE SHOW
AT THE PARIS OPERA!
FIRST NITERS. (*Sing.*)
DRESSING FOR THE PRIDE, FOR THE "GLOIRE DE
  LA FRANCE"
DRESSING UP TO GO
TO THE PARIS OPERA!
ACTORS.
PARIS OPERA!
FIRST NITERS. (*As more appear.*)
IT'S A NEW SEASON AND THAT'S THE REASON
WE BUY THESE CLOTHES BY THE ROW ...
ACTORS.
DRESSING FOR THE FUN, FOR THE LIGHTS, FOR
  THE GLARE ...
FIRST NITERS.
DRESSING UP TO PREEN AT THE PARIS OPERA!
ACTORS.
DRESSING TO DESCEND ON A CLOUD ON A
  STAIR ...
FIRST NITERS.
DRESSING TO BE SEEN AT THE PARIS OPERA!
PARIS OPERA!
EVERYONE WILL BE THERE!
ALL. (*As more of each group appear.*)
EVERYONE WILL BE THERE,
EVERYONE ... !
ACTORS.
THE CORPS DE BALLET!
WE ACTORS WILL PLAY!
OUR SET SO SPECTACULAR AND GRAND!
FIRST NITERS.
ARRIVE SOMEWHAT LATE

MAKE SURE THAT YOU ATE
EXPECT EVERYONE TO UNDERSTAND!
  ACTORS.
WITH BREATHLESS SURPRISE
THE CURTAIN WILL RISE
STEP OUT WITH A GESTURE OF THE HAND ...
  FIRST NITERS.
LOOK THROUGH THE LORGNETTE
AND DO NOT FORGET
JAMAIS! NEVER LISTEN TO THE BAND!
  ALL.
DRESSING FOR THE NIGHT,
FOR THE BALL, FOR THE SHOW,
DRESSING UP TO GO TO THE
PARIS OPERA! PARIS OPERA!

(*Continuing, as the ACTORS raise masks to their faces, the FIRST NITERS hold up champagne glasses, lorgnettes, open fans, and in one case affect a monocle.*)

PAREE! PAREE IS A MASK
WHATEVER YOU ASK SHE'LL BE FOR YOU
PAREE! ONE NIGHT AT MAXIMS
A GLORIOUS DREAM, A RENDEZVOUS!
A NIGHT AT THE OPERA, TRIP TO THE BALLET,
EVENING OF THEATRE, ALL IN A DAY ...
PAREE! ONE VIEW IN THE MIST,
AND YOU HAVE BEEN KISSED FROM FAR AWAY...

DRESSING FOR THE NIGHT,
FOR THE BALL, FOR THE SHOW
DRESSING UP TO GO TO THE
PARIS OPERA! PARIS OPERA!
  CHRISTINE. (*Still "in the street."*)
PAREE IS THE RAIN ...

FIRST NITERS.
PAREE IS A MASK
THE PHANTOM. (*Still in his "lair."*)
PAREE IS THE NIGHT—FOR ME ...
ACTORS/FIRST NITERS.
DRESSING FOR THE NIGHT,
FOR THE BALL, FOR THE SHOW,
FOR THE BALL, FOR THE NIGHT, FOR THE
  SHOW...
ALL.
PAREE!
  (*Spoken.*) Paree!

(*The song ends. THE PHANTOM and CHRISTINE
disappear from view. [Music Cue #3A: POST
OPENING] GERARD CARRIERE, an old, elegant,
kindly man, emerges from the crowd in shock. ALAIN
CHOLET, an excessively dapper man, and his
imperious wife, the diva, LA CARLOTTA, are with
him.*)

CARRIERE. ... But you can't do this! I *must* stay
on! I have demands, obligations you don't know about!
  CHOLET. (*With an unctuous smile.*) I'm sorry.
  CARLOTTA. I'm sure you've done a wonderful job.

(*CARLOTTA laughs and strolls regally with CHOLET to
other First Niters. The MINISTER OF CULTURE, a
haughty man in a very expensive coat, sidles past
Carriere.*)

MINISTER OF CULTURE. (*To Carriere, sotto
voce.*) And we'd like you out of here tonight.

(*MEMBERS OF THE COMPANY rush over to
CARRIERE, who is reeling from the news.*)

OPERA TENOR. Monsieur Carriere, what is it?
FLEURE. What's happened?
CARRIERE. (*Dazed.*) I've just been dismissed.
OPERA TENOR. NO! NO!
SECOND DIVA. It's not possible!
FLORA. How could they have done this?

(*CARRIERE shrugs helplessly. His FRIENDS glare at Cholet and Carlotta.*)

FLORENCE. I bet they *bought* their way in!
SECOND TENOR. How else?

(*The MINISTER OF CULTURE moves forward.*)

SECOND DIVA. And there's the man they bribed—the Minister of Culture.
FLORENCE. Sub-culture is more like it.
MINISTER OF CULTURE. (*To the company.*) Dear Friends ... (*His words are greeted by a chorus of BOOS and HISSES. HE quiets them.*) Please! I understand your disappointment. Gerard Carriere has been a part of our lives for years, a truly great managing director, and his retirement distresses me deeply. (*More BOOS and HISSES. HE quiets them down with a gesture.*) My colleagues, cherished patrons, I give you your new managing director, Alain Cholet. (*Tepid APPLAUSE as CHOLET bows.*) And, of course, his very talented wife ... (*The MINISTER leans toward Cholet.*)
CHOLET. (*Sotto voce.*) Carlotta.
MINISTER OF CULTURE. (*To the company.*) Carlotta!

(*CARLOTTA moves forward grandly to even more tepid APPLAUSE.*)

CHOLET. (*To the company, grandly.*) This is a moment we will never forget!

[Music Cue #3B: FALLING NOTE MUSIC]

(Suddenly, a NOTE flutters down. ALL look up! Some SCREAM, others begin to SCATTER.)

VARIOUS PEOPLE. It's the Phantom! / The Phantom!
CHOLET. ... Phantom?
OPERA TENOR. They didn't tell you?
CHOLET. Tell me what?
MINISTER OF CULTURE. (*To Cholet, hastily.*) Nothing. It's just a rumor.

(The PERSON who retrieved the note hurries with it to Carriere.)

MAN WITH NOTE. It's for you.

(CARRIERE reads the note, crumples it and puts it in his pocket.)

CHOLET. What is going on?
CARRIERE. (*Grim look.*) I'll explain in my office.
CHOLET. You mean *my* office.
CARRIERE. Of course. Forgive me.

(THEY exit. The place is in turmoil.)

CARLOTTA. ... Phantom?
MINISTER OF CULTURE. Really, it's just a rumor.

(The Manager's office appears. CHOLET and CARRIERE enter. All else is gone.)

CARRIERE. Who is Joseph Buquet?

CHOLET. My wife's costume man. She sent him to take an inventory of what's down below.

CARRIERE. I think he may have found something he wasn't looking for. (*HE hands CHOLET the mysterious note.*)

CHOLET. (*Reads.*) "Joseph Buquet broke the rules." (*Looking up at Carriere.*) ... *What* rules?"

CARRIERE. You mean no one told you?

CHOLET. ... About what?

CARRIERE. This Opera House. It's haunted.

CHOLET. ... "*Haunted*?"

CARRIERE. By a ghost.

CHOLET. *What*!?

CARRIERE. This ghost has certain rules, which must be obeyed. If they are, everything is fine. Obviously, your wife's costume man didn't know the rules.

CHOLET. Carriere...

CARRIERE.
  "All you need to know
  Is don't go down below."

CHOLET. What's that?

CARRIERE. The rules.

CHOLET. Carriere, if this is a joke, it isn't funny.

CARRIERE. It's no joke. This ghost has been here as long as I. But we obeyed his rules, so all went well. Rumor has it he lives by the edge of a lagoon, at the lowest level of the Opera House, attended by a colony of lost souls. During the days of the Paris Commune there were torture chambers down there. That's his domain. And anyone who goes down there does not return ... He calls himself "the Phantom of the Opera."

CHOLET. Carriere, I do not believe a word of this. This is a ploy, designed by you to get back at me and my wife for having had you fired. *I do not believe in ghosts*!

(HE storms out. CARRIERE stares after him in gloom.)

THE PHANTOM'S VOICE. *What is going on?*
CARRIERE. *(Seems not at all surprised by the voice.)* Is he dead?
THE PHANTOM'S VOICE. Answer my question.
CARRIERE. ERIK!
THE PHANTOM'S VOICE. Yes, he's dead!

(CARRIERE, with a hopeless sigh, shuts his eyes.)

THE PHANTOM'S VOICE. They were *warned*! The man went where he shouldn't! *I had no choice!*
CARRIERE. Of course you did. You could have let him go.
THE PHANTOM'S VOICE. If I had, he'd have gone right back up. And they'd be down after me in a second. He found out where I live. *And he saw my face!*

[Music Cue #4: HE SAW MY FACE]

CARRIERE. Oh God.

(A panel in the wall slides open.
Dark doorway.)

THE PHANTOM'S VOICE. *(Soft, insistent.)* *Come in.*

(CARRIERE walks through. The panel slides shut.
As it does, the office moves aside and reveals a dark network of corridors built of stone—a dungeon of a place. THE PHANTOM is standing there, the mask on his face expressing rage.)

THE PHANTOM. All my life, I have lived by threatening to kill. Now it's finally happened. Why did you let him go *down* there!?

CARRIÈRE. I didn't know he was *going* down.

THE PHANTOM. But it's your *JOB* to know!

CARRIERE. I've been replaced.

THE PHANTOM. (*Gasps*.)... *Replaced*?

CARRIERE. I didn't learn about it till just now. That's why all this happened.

THE PHANTOM. Well! ... What a day of surprises *this* is turning out to be! (*HE paces about; thrown. Finally, HE stops and stares at the old man.*) This man who's replacing you ... (*Hopefully.*) ...does he, per chance, believe in ghosts?

CARRIERE. No.

THE PHANTOM. *What am I to do*?

CARRIERE. (*Barely audible.*) I'm not sure.

THE PHANTOM. I will have to *make* him believe, that's what!

CARRIERE. I'm afraid that won't be so easy. I just tried.

THE PHANTOM. ... It's all changed now, hasn't it?

CARRIERE. At best I had a few more years. Surely you must have known!

THE PHANTOM. I had rather hoped you'd be able to pick your successor.

CARRIERE. Ahhhhh ... Yes ... So had I.

(*The enormity of it all is only just now really hitting the PHANTOM.*)

THE PHANTOM. (*Lost, almost like a child.*) ... What's to become of me?

CARRIERE. I don't know.

(The PHANTOM looks about, lost. HE sees some of his acolytes. THEY turn away and cower, as if shaken by the news. CARRIERE sees them, too.)

CARRIERE. *(To Erik, re the acolytes.)* You have *them.* Maybe *they* can help.
THE PHANTOM. With what? They can hardly help themselves. If I didn't get them food every now and then, they'd starve.

(Suddenly, a soprano's VOICE is heard, distantly, vocalizing. The VOICE is remarkably awful.)

THE PHANTOM. ... My God! The place really *is* haunted!

(CARRIERE laughs. THE PHANTOM walks to a section of the corridor and pulls back a panel. A hole of LIGHT can be seen. The VOICE is louder. HE peeks through the hole.
A moment later, HE turns to Carriere, puzzled.)

THE PHANTOM. Who *is* this?
CARRIERE. Without looking, I would say, Carlotta.
THE PHANTOM. And who is she?
CARRIERE. A new member of the company.
THE PHANTOM. But she can't sing!
CARRIERE. Obviously, that is something she doesn't know.
THE PHANTOM. Well, someone should TELL her!
CARRIERE. That's not so easy. She's married to the new manager.
THE PHANTOM. Good God! This means she's probably going to sing all the time! *(Wryly.)* *What kind of ho or are you leaving e in!?*

CARRIERE. This is not my doing!

THE PHANTOM. (*Straight; sympathetic.*) I know that. (*Suddenly, an idea occurs.*) ... You say she's married to the new manager?

CARRIERE. Yes.

THE PHANTOM. I know what to do. (*Sly grin.*) I'll *kill* them.

CARRIERE. Erik!

THE PHANTOM. Come-come, I'm teasing. Probably the only one I need to kill is her.

CARRIERE. Oh my God.

THE PHANTOM. *What has happened to your humor?*

CARRIERE. *My* humor?

THE PHANTOM. You're right. Sorry. I'm not used to killing people. It's thrown me off a bit!

(CARLOTTA sings a high, wobbly trill.)

THE PHANTOM. ...You know what? I think her voice is worse than my face.

(SHE continues to vocalize. It's so bad now it seems to hurt his ears.)

THE PHANTOM. I can't live hearing sounds like that! I need some beauty! You know that! (*HE tries to shut out her sound but can't.*) ... I suppose she'll be choosing the opera season too.

CARRIERE. I gather she intends to run everything.

THE PHANTOM. I have it! *I'm coming with you!*

CARRIERE. Erik ...

THE PHANTOM. Ahhhh! But I can't, can I? Sometimes I forget that I am fit for nowhere but these gloomy vaults. Bereaved of light. Like darkness itself. For I *am* darkness itself, aren't I? Where are my golden tents? Where are my lambs, rejoicing?

(The PHANTOM stares at Carriere. HE makes a sharp gesture of dismissal. The ACOLYTES lead CARRIERE out. MUSIC.)

[Music Cue # 5: WHERE IN THE WORLD]

THE PHANTOM. *(Sings.)*
WHERE IS THE PATH THAT LEADS OUT FROM
    THIS PLACE
NOW THAT ALL HAS BEEN CHANGED ON THIS
    DAY?
WHERE IS THE SENSE OF THE LIFE THAT I LEAD
NOW THAT MUSIC'S BEEN TAKEN AWAY?

WHY WAS I BORN TO THIS GRAVE,
LANGUISHING DEEP IN THIS TOMB?
OH FOR AN ANGEL OF MUSIC TO COME
AND RESTORE A SMALL GLIMMER OF LIGHT TO
    MY GLOOM …

WHERE IN THE WORLD
IN THE VAST OPEN WORLD
IS A VOICE THAT CAN SING?

EVERY NOTE BUILDING HIGH
LETTING FREE, LETTING FLY
LIKE A BIRD TAKING WING!

WHERE IN THE WORLD
IF IT CAN BE,
WHERE IS SHE?

WHAT LITTLE TOWN
HIDES A GIRL IN A GOWN
WITH A THROAT LIKE A LARK?

WITH A VOICE THAT IS STRONG
WHO, WITH EFFORTLESS SONG
MAKES A LIGHT IN THE DARK?

WHERE IN THE WORLD?
WHERE IN THE WORLD?

NOT A DAY I'LL REST
TILL THAT VOICE IS FOUND ...

SEARCH ON THE QUAYS
IN THE STREETS, THE CAFÉS
FIND THE ONE I DESIRE!

YOU WILL KNOW SHE IS NEAR
BY A WARMTH IN YOUR EAR
AND YOUR SOUL CATCHING FIRE...
OUT IN THE WORLD, SOMEWHERE!

SHE WHO WAS BORN TO COMMAND
BY SINGING!

SHE WITH THE TONE OF A BELL
THE WIND IS RINGING!

AND SHE WHO WILL HARDLY SUSPECT
WHAT SHE IS BRINGING
TO A PLAN I WEAVE WITH GRAND DESIGN.

GO IN THE WORLD
DON'T RETURN FROM THE WORLD
TILL YOU FIND ME THE ONE ...

WITH THE STANCE OF A QUEEN
AND AN EYE AS SERENE
AND AS BRIGHT AS THE SUN CAN SHINE!

FIND IN THE WORLD
THIS MIRAGE THAT I SEE
AND FROM THE WORLD
YOU WILL BRING HER TO ME
AND I'LL MAKE HER MINE.

[Music Cue #5A: INTRODUCTION OF CHRISTINE]

*(LIGHTS UP on the backstage area, by the Stage Door.
CHRISTINE, who has just entered, is standing with
JEAN-CLAUDE, an old, crusty Stage Door Man.
Simultaneously, the PHANTOM fades from view.)*

CHRISTINE. I'm supposed to see a Monsieur
Gerard Carriere. I believe he's the manager. The Count
de Chandon sent me. He said Monsieur Carriere could
arrange for me to have singing lessons. *(SHE nervously
holds out the Count's business card.)*
JEAN-CLAUDE. Monsieur Carriere has just been
fired.
CHRISTINE. *Fired?*

*(SHE stares out in shock. HE walks off to attend to other
matters. CHRISTINE looks around, dreams dashed.
FLORA, FLORENCE and FLEURE—long-time
members of the chorus known for gossiping—who
have been watching from the periphery, grin at each
other knowingly and approach the forlorn Christine
with mischievous glee. EACH of the three wears a
heart-shaped locket.)*

FLORENCE. *(Feigning innocence.)* Dear. By any
chance, did the Count de Chandon send you here?
CHRISTINE. *(Turns to them with an eager, hopeful
smile.)* Yes! Do you know him?

(THEY open their lockets.)

FLEURE. Is this him?

(CHRISTINE stares at their lockets in astonishment. SHE nods weakly.)

FLORA. (*To her cohorts.*) And I thought he loved only *me*!

(FLORENCE and FLEURE barely suppress their laughter.)

FLORENCE. Dear, we're curious—where did he find you?
CHRISTINE. On the street.
FLORENCE. (*To her cohorts.*) He's getting desperate!

(THEY giggle.)

FLEURE. Let me guess. Did he tell you you had nice legs?
CHRISTINE. Nice *legs*? ... No. No, he heard me singing.
FLORA. And thought you had a nice *voice*.
CHRISTINE. Yes!
FLORENCE. And asked if you'd like lessons.

*(CHRISTINE nods. The WOMEN giggle.
FLORENCE and FLEURE start off.)*

CHRISTINE. Are you *all* friends of his?
FLORA. Yes!

(SHE nods in a way CHRISTINE doesn't like. SHE saunters off, giggling and joins the other two.

CHRISTINE *stars after them in dismay, then struggling against tears, turns towards the Stage Door and starts to leave. JEAN-CLAUDE, who has seen all this, rushes over to her.)*

JEAN-CLAUDE. Mademoiselle! Maybe the new manager can help. Not promising anything. Come on.

(JEAN-CLAUDE exits with CHRISTINE.
The scene shifts. The MANAGER'S OFFICE glides on. [The manager's office is a suite and will serve as Carlotta and Cholet's new home.]
The place has undergone a startling change. Carlotta has had her "things" moved in: A RACK OF CLOTHES, A STEAMER TRUNK, and PORTRAITS OF HERSELF. Basically these portraits are all the same— same expression, same pose. Only the costumes change. These are the costumes of the great opera roles.
At rise, CARLOTTA is with CHOLET. And SHE is furious.)

CHOLET. ... A *ghost*?
CARLOTTA. Yes. In my dressing room!
CHOLET. How do you know?
CARLOTTA. Because the lights FLICKERED!
CHOLET. That doesn't mean it was a *ghost*.
CARLOTTA. (*Leaning closer, scared.*) I heard *odd* sounds ... from *behind the walls* ... (*Worst news of all.*) ... while I was *vocalizing*.
CHOLET. Maybe it was rats.
CARLOTTA. Sounded to me like *snickering*.

(CHOLET ponders, puzzled.
A beat.)

CARLOTTA. Then, my dressing table rose.

CHOLET. ... "Rose?"

CARLOTTA. And knocked me over. (*Beat.*) My costumes fell off the wall. (*Beat.*) And I heard that distinctive snickering *again*.

CHOLET. (*Cold smile; he's got the answer.*) My dear, *this is not the work of a ghost.*

CARLOTTA. (*Real panic setting in.*) You mean, this is what these dressing rooms are *like*?

CHOLET. No-no! I mean, this is simply a plot.

CARLOTTA. (*Incredulous.*) ... Against *me*?

CHOLET. Against US!

CARLOTTA. (*Utter disbelief.*) Who would want to plot against us?

CHOLET. Carriere! The former manager. I met with him before. The man is crazed with fury at our having fired him.

CARLOTTA. Ahhhhh ... !

CHOLET. Don't worry. I'll take care of it. Nothing to worry about. Addio!

CARLOTTA. Addio!

(*CHOLET chuckles, opens the door and exits. In so doing, VARIOUS MEMBERS OF THE STAFF walk in with samples of their work: swatches of materials, set designs, models.*)

CARLOTTA. Who are *you*?

ONE OF THE STAFF. Your new staff.

ANOTHER MEMBER OF THE STAFF. Here to show you what we have planned for the new season.

CARLOTTA. What *you* have planned!!!?

(*THEY back away.*)

CARLOTTA. When I am ready, I will tell you what *I* have planned! What *I*!!! ... have planned. (*Icily sweet.*) Do you see the difference?

(THEY nod.)

CARLOTTA. Good. Now get out! *Out! OUT!* I
have a thousand things to do!
THE STAFF. *(Speaking at the same time; utter chaos.)*
But madame... / We need to show you—! / We have
these wonderful sketches! / Perhaps you don't quite
realize—!
CARLOTTA. OUT! *GET OUT!*

(THEY exit hastily. MUSIC.)

[Music Cue #6: THIS PLACE IS MINE]

CARLOTTA. *(Sings.)*
WHERE DOES THE TIME FLY?
SIMPLY TOO FEW HOURS IN THE DAY!

OH A DIVA'S WORK IS NEVER DONE
NO RELIEF, NO TIME FOR FUN
NOT IF THE DIVA HAS TO RUN
AN OPERA COMPANY.

EVERY SMALL DETAIL TO SUPERVISE
EVERY PRETTY FACE TO SCRU------TINIZE
I PLAN BENEATH THESE EYES
THIS OPERA COMPANY.

WHY TAKE ON THIS ARDUOUS CHORE?
SLEEPLESS NIGHTS I PACE ACROSS MY
    BEDROOM FLOOR
WHY DO I LIVE COMPLETELY FOR THIS OPERA
    COMPANY?

'CAUSE IT'S MINE, FROM THE STALLS TO THE
    PORTRAITS ON THE WALLS

TO THE BALCONIES AND LOGES FAR AND NEAR.
IT BELONGS ALL TO ME, EVERY ITEM THAT YOU
   SEE FROM THE
CELLAR TO THE CRYSTAL CHANDELIER.
FROM THE FLUTED MARBLE GRANDE FACADE
   TO THE ELEVATED PROMENADE
FROM EVERY TOILET BOWL—TO EVERY
   LEADING ROLE
THIS PLACE IS MINE!

I WILL SING, I WILL GLOW, I WILL NEVER LET IT
   GO
I WILL HOLD IT EVER CAPTIVE IN MY HAND.
LIKE A GOD, LIKE A QUEEN, I WILL ENTER ANY
   SCENE
AND CONTROL IT LIKE A KINGDOM I COMMAND.
AND I PITY ANY BARITONE, WHO ATTEMPTS TO
   TREAD THE STAGE I OWN
WITH NO POLITE REQUEST ... HE'S HERE AT MY
   BEHEST
'CAUSE IT'S ALL MINE!

MY CURTAIN AND MY CANOPY
MY SONG, MY KEY, MY CHART.
MY GRAND ROMANTIC DESTINY
FROM HERE MY LIFE WILL START ...

I'LL BE OUT ON THE STAGE, LOOKING GREAT
   AND HALF MY AGE
EVERY CHANCE I GET, I'LL GET 'EM ON THEIR
   FEET!
I WILL BURN, I WILL SCHEME, I WILL REALIZE
   MY DREAM
'CAUSE IF I'M NOT IN A LIGHT I'M INCOMPLETE.
AND THE BEST PART I'M JUST COMING TO,
HOW THEY'LL ALL APPLAUD FOR YOU-KNOW-
   WHO

I CAN'T BELIEVE I'M HERE—AND THIS IS *MY* CAREER!

IT MUST BE SEEN, LIKE A TORCH
WE'LL ENGRAVE IT ON THE PORCH!
LIKE AN EDICT, LIKE A BEACON, LIKE A SIGN!

(The suite "breaks open" part sliding off in one direction, the other part in another as the hanger flies out. At the same time various MEMBERS OF THE COMPANY enter and take their places for a freeze on the final note of her song.)

CARLOTTA.
THIS PLACE IS MINE!

(CHOLET, with CHRISTINE and JEAN-CLAUDE, are in another part of the backstage area.)

CHOLET. *Lessons*?

(CHRISTINE nods.)

JEAN-CLAUDE. She was sent by the Count de Chandon.
CHOLET. (*Imperiously unimpressed.*) And who is the Count de Chandon?
JEAN-CLAUDE. (*Sotto voce.*) Heir to a champagne fortune and the opera's biggest patron.
CHOLET. Ahhhhh!
CHRISTINE. Here's his card.
CHOLET. (*Reading from the card.*) "Give this girl lessons." (*To Christine, with new-found interest.*) Well! I'm sure we can find something.

*(HE leads CHRISTINE over to a mirror where
   CARLOTTA is holding up a dress overdone to an
   extreme.)*

CHOLET. (*On entering.*) Darling! This lovely young
girl would like singing lessons. What can we do?
CARLOTTA. Nothing! You think this girl can sing?
Look at how she stands. Look at what she's wearing!
Where did you grow up, on a *farm*?
CHRISTINE. (*Shyly.*) ... Yes.
CARLOTTA. The world of opera has nothing to do
with farm life! (*To her husband, crossly.*) Why are you
asking me this?
CHOLET. (*Sotto voce.*) She has a patron who's
powerful.
CARLOTTA. Ahhhhh ... ! (*To Christine.*) There is
one way to learn to sing. *Observe singers*! My dear, I am
going to do you a favor. I am going let you work for *me*!
... In the costume department. (*To Cholet.*) She has just
replaced Joseph Buquet. Who seems to have disappeared.

(CHOLET stares at her, startled.)

JEAN-CLAUDE. (*To Christine.*) Come. I'll get you
set up.

*(HE hurries to lead CHRISTINE out, as if afraid Carlotta
   might change her mind and the deal get even worse.)*

JEAN-CLAUDE. (*To Christine, as THEY exit,
sotto voce.*) I know it's not exactly what you wanted ...
CHRISTINE. Oh no! Really. It's wonderful. I
mean, just to be *around* this place ... !

*(THEY exit. CARLOTTA resumes primping by the
   mirror. CHOLET looks on.)*

CARLOTTA. All right. The truth. How do I look?

CHOLET. You look like spring. No, better—you look like a *young* spring. Like a spring that is not yet *even* spring. That is *about* to be spring. That is winter! (*Seeing her expression change.*) No-no! It is *not* winter. It is spring. Definitely spring.

CARLOTTA. You wouldn't lie to me, would you?

CHOLET. No-no. Never!

(*THEY kiss—several times. Then CHOLET starts off and CARLOTTA follows him past CHRISTINE who is attending to the costumes on the rack of costumes. SHE stops and turns back to Christine.*)

CARLOTTA. Yes! That's it! Good, very good! The only way to learn to sing ... !

(*CARLOTTA turns and exits.*
[Music Cue #7: HOME]
A few MEMBERS of the company enter and drop more costumes for Christine to collect. THEY pay her no heed.
To Christine, the fact that the theatre is empty now is wonderful. SHE smiles like a child left alone in a great toy store.
MUSIC builds—very dreamlike.)

CHRISTINE. (*Sings.*)
ALL MY LIFE I'VE BEEN WAITING
IN MY MIND, IN A ROCKING CHAIR
FOR MY FANCY TO TAKE THE AIR
I WOULD KNOW THE TIME.

TICK AND TOCK WENT MY CHILDHOOD
FATHER SAID I WOULD KNOW THE PLACE
SKIN WOULD TINGLE, AND PULSE WOULD RACE
AS THEY DO...

IT'S HERE!
I'M...

HOME, WHERE MUSIC FILLS THE AIR, AND I'M
HOME, WHERE A THOUSAND LOVERS CRY
SWOON AND SIGH, AND I'M
HOME, WHERE EVERY VIOLIN
PLAYS A TREAT
AS SWEET AS A HONEYCOMB.
WHEREVER MUSIC PLAYS
I KNOW
I'M HOME.

HERE, WHERE FABLES COME ALIVE
YEAR BY YEAR
WE FORGET OUR TROUBLED NIGHTS
UNDER LIGHTS
AND EACH TEAR BECOMES A GENTLE TUNE
OR DUET
KEPT STRAIGHT BY A METRONOME...
AND IF I'M SINGING, THEN I KNOW
I'M HOME.

WHERE EVERY ENGLISH HORN
MAKES ME FEEL GLAD I'M BORN.
AND ANY WOODWIND TRILL
EXCITES A THRILL THAT'S NEW!

THE GIANT CONTRABASS...
THE GREAT SOPRANO'S FACE
COMBINE TO MAKE A PERFECT WORLD
FAR BETTER THAN WHAT'S OUTSIDE.

DREAMS—I'VE LIVED WITHIN MY DREAMS
NOW IT SEEMS I'VE AWAKENED
AND THEY'RE REAL
PINCH AND FEEL!

IF ONE DAY
I WALK UPON THIS STAGE FROM THESE WINGS
AND PLAY UNDERNEATH THIS DOME,
AND IF I SING WITH ALL MY HEART ... I'LL BE
HOME.

*(The LIGHTS come up on the PHANTOM, down below.
Christine's VOICE has filtered down. HE hears, and,
    drawn by the sound, begins to ascend.)*

THE PHANTOM.
ALL MY LIFE TO BE WAITING
FOR AN ANGEL TO ONE DAY SPEAK
MOUTH GOES DRY, AND MY KNEES GROW
    WEAK
AT EACH WORD—EACH SOUND—

THAT VOICE—THAT MUSIC IN THE AIR
EVERY CHOICE, EVERY SYLLABLE
EACH NOTE—HOW THEY FLOAT
AND HER TONE! A MIRACLE OF SILK, SPUN TO
    GOLD
UNFOLDING IN POLYCHROME ...
AND WHEN I HEAR IT HOW I KNOW
I'M HOME.

*(CHRISTINE goes off to get a clothes hamper to collect
    the costumes which have been dropped on stage. As
    the PHANTOM sings, SHE returns.)*

THE PHANTOM.
WHO IS THIS PRODIGY
WHO SINGS TO ONLY ME?
SHE IS AS INNOCENT
AND NATURAL AS A ROSE.
I'LL DO HER SO MUCH GOOD
WE TWO, I KNOW WE COULD

COMBINE TO MAKE A PERFECT WORLD
FAR BETTER THAN WHAT'S OUTSIDE.

*(The PHANTOM emerges from the shadows behind her
    and THEY sing together, but not to each other.)*

DREAMS (MY DREAMS)
I'VE LIVED WITHIN MY DREAMS
NOW IT SEEMS I'VE AWAKENED AND THEY'RE
    REAL
IF THEY'RE REAL ...
IF ONE DAY
I (SHE) WALK (WALKS) UPON THIS STAGE
FROM THESE WINGS
AND PLAY (PLAYS) UNDERNEATH
THIS DOME, AND IF I (SHE) SINGS
WITH ALL MY (HER) HEART
I'LL BE ... HOME.

[Music Cue #8: PHANTOM'S MONOLOGUE]

THE PHANTOM. (*Softly, warmly.*) Mademoiselle
... (*SHE starts.*) Please. Don't be afraid. I am a friend.
As well as an admirer. (*SHE tries to see him.*) No,
please! I would appreciate it greatly if you would be so
kind as to just stay where you are. (*SHE stops.*) Thank
you. I have my reasons. ... Mademoiselle, just now I
heard you sing. (*CHRISTINE stares back, startled.*) I
know, you thought you were alone. You were not.
Mademoiselle, the truth is, your voice is astonishing. An
angel's voice! Exquisite in every detail, except ... (*HE
seems scared by what he is about to say.*) ... It is
untrained. Without training, your voice will never attain
the heights for which I know it has been destined. I ...
would like to help bring you there. And I can! I am
myself a singer of ... some renown. (*CHRISTINE starts
moving closer.*) No-no, stay there. There is a condition.

And it is inviolable. I have never taken on any students, for until just now I have never wanted to. If others hear that I am giving lessons, they will want them as well. Therefore, if you choose to let me be your guide in this, as I dearly hope you will, I must insist that I remain ... *anonymous.* (*Pause.*) And I will do so by wearing a *mask.* Please, there's no need for an answer now. I will find *you* ... *Au revoir.*

(*HE disappears into the shadows. SHE stares toward the shadows, stunned.*)

CHRISTINE. (*Sings.*)
AND IF I SING WITH ALL MY HEART,
I'LL BE ...

[Music Cue #9: CHOLET/LEDOUX]

(*SHE exits with clothes rack.
LIGHTS cross-fade and INSPECTOR LEDOUX, head of the Paris police, and CHOLET enter. In the background, STAGEHANDS are moving scenery from* Aida. *Members of the company are in Egyptian costume; a rehearsal is in progress.*)

CHOLET. Inspector Ledoux! Thank you so much for coming.
LEDOUX. My pleasure.

(*CHOLET takes LEDOUX off to a side where Carlotta can't overhear.*)

CHOLET. (*As THEY walk—sotto voce, nervous.*) Personally, I don't believe in ghosts myself you understand.
LEDOUX. I understand.
CHOLET. It's my *wife* I'm trying to reassure!

(HE checks CARLOTTA, but SHE pays no heed; SHE's too busy watching the set-up for Aida *and adjusting her wig.)*

LEDOUX. Monsieur, these "infamous letters"— where are they?

CHOLET. Right here. (*HE takes out a packet of letters.*) Listen to this one! Just arrived. "*Aida* is a fine opera and I approve of its selection. What I do *not* approve of is your wife being in it." *Does not approve of my wife being in it*! This is her Paris debut! The most important moment of her career! And the Phantom of the Opera does not APPROVE!?

LEDOUX. Monsieur, it is only a note.

CHOLET. From a *ghost*!? Since when do ghosts write? And this has been going on all month! Every day! Insults and demands! And every note signed, "The Phantom of the Opera."

LEDOUX. Monsieur, the Phantom of the Opera has never bothered anyone.

CHOLET. Well, this is bothering US! My wife is extremely sensitive! She needs to know that people *love* her!

LEDOUX. Then why worry? These are from a ghost.

CHOLET. Ledoux, don't you understand? There *is* no ghost! These are from the former manager, a snake named Carriere!

LEDOUX. Monsieur ...

CHOLET. I want him arrested!

LEDOUX. On what charge?

CHOLET. Criticizing my wife's performance before she has even performed!

(LEDOUX sighs. The MUSIC changes.

*LIGHTS DOWN on the stage and UP on a SECRET
MUSIC ROOM. The PHANTOM is at a piano,
CHRISTINE stands nearby.
It's NIGHT. LIGHTS are from candles.)*

[Music Cue #10: PHANTOM FUGUE PART I]

THE PHANTOM. All right. We begin. Repeat after
me, singing on the syllable "la." (*HE sings.*)
LA LA LA LA LA LA LA
LA LA LA LA LA LA LA
LA LA LA LA LA LA LA
LA LA LA LA LA LA LA LA
    CHRISTINE.
LA LA LA LA LA LA LA
LA LA LA LA LA LA LA
LA LA LA LA LA LA LA
LA LA LA LA LA LA LA LA
    THE PHANTOM. Now ... "Ba."
BA BA BA BA BA BA BA
BA BA BA BA BA BA BA
BA BA BA BA BA BA BA
BA BA BA BA BA BA BA BA
    CHRISTINE.
BA BA BA BA BA BA BA
BA BA BA BA BA BA BA
BA BA BA BA BA BA BA
BA BA BA BA BA BA BA BA
    THE PHANTOM. (*Arpeggios.*)
LA LA LA LA LA LA
LA LA LA LA LA LA
LA LA LA LA LA LA
LA LA LA LA LA LA
    CHRISTINE. (*Arpeggios.*)
LA LA LA LA LA LA
LA LA LA LA LA LA
LA LA LA LA LA LA

LA LA LA LA LA LA

(The LIGHTS shift to the Manager's office.)

LEDOUX. *(To Cholet.)* You mean, ... *Aida* is not *supposed* to be funny?
CHOLET. Oh, the reviews! ... the reviews!
FIRST POLICEMEN. We've discovered how it happened. Bugs.
CHOLET. ... "Bugs"?
FIRST POLICEMAN. Yes. The wig is *infested*!
SECOND POLICEMAN. Some prankster must have put them there! *(To Carlotta, brightly.)* That's why you kept scratching during your arias!

(CARLOTTA screams. LIGHTS shift to the Music Room.)

THE PHANTOM.
LA LA LA LA LA LA LA
LA LA LA LA LA LA LA
LA LA LA LA LA LA LA
LA LA LA LA LA LA LA LA
  CHRISTINE.
LA LA LA LA LA LA LA
LA LA LA LA LA LA LA
LA LA LA LA LA LA LA
LA LA LA LA LA LA LA LA
  THE PHANTOM.
BA BA BA BA BA BA BA
BA BA BA BA BA BA BA
BA BA BA BA BA BA BA
BA BA BA BA BA BA BA BA
  CHRISTINE.
BA BA BA BA BA BA BA
BA BA BA BA BA BA BA
BA BA BA BA BA BA BA

BA BA BA BA BA BA BA BA

(LIGHTS change again. We're back in the Manager's office.)

LEDOUX. You mean, *La Traviata* is not supposed to be funny *either*?
CARLOTTA. *(Double.)* Ohhhhh!
CHOLET. *Correct.*
FIRST POLICEMAN. We've figured out how the trick was done.
SECOND POLICEMAN. Glue.
CHOLET. ... *Glue*?
FIRST POLICEMAN. Glue. Yes. So when madam took the glass to give a toast ...? *(The FIRST POLICEMAN holds up a goblet on a tray. HE holds it by the goblet's stem. The tray is glued to the goblet.)*
SECOND POLICEMAN. Ordinary "glue"!
CARLOTTA. *(Double.)* AGGGHHH!

(LIGHTS change back to the Music Room.)

CHRISTINE.
LA LA LA LA LA LA LA
LA LA LA LA LA LA LA
LA LA LA LA LA LA LA
LA LA LA LA LA LA LA LA
   THE PHANTOM.
LA LA LA LA LA LA LA
LA LA LA LA LA LA LA
LA LA LA LA LA LA LA
LA LA LA LA LA LA LA LA
   THE PHANTOM.
BA BA BA BA BA BA BA
BA BA BA BA BA BA BA
BA BA BA BA BA BA BA
BA BA BA BA BA BA BA BA

CHRISTINE.
BA BA BA BA BA BA BA
BA BA BA BA BA BA BA
BA BA BA BA BA BA BA
BA BA BA BA BA BA BA BA
   THE PHANTOM. (*Arpeggios.*)
LA LA LA LA LA LA
LA LA LA LA LA LA
LA LA LA LA LA LA
LA LA LA LA LA LA
   CHRISTINE. (*Arpeggios.*)
LA LA LA LA LA LA
LA LA LA LA LA LA
LA LA LA LA LA LA
LA LA LA LA LA LA

(*LIGHTS switch again to Manager's office.*)

   CHOLET. ... Would you like a drink?
   CARLOTTA. Yes. Something mixed with hemlock.
   CHOLET. (*To Ledoux, attempting a laugh.*) I'll get her a brandy. (*HE heads for an armoire.*)
   LEDOUX. (*Reading from some newspapers.*) No. You're right. These reviews are definitely not good.

(*CARLOTTA heaves a mournful sob.*
CHOLET opens the armoire. Inside, is Joseph Buquet's corpse, propped upright. CHOLET screams.)

   CHOLET. J-J-J-Joseph ... B-B-B-Buquet!

(*ALL of them gasp.*)

   CARLOTTA. (*In horror.*) My costume man!
   CHOLET. (*To Ledoux.*) She sent him down below!
   LEDOUX. Well, someone has sent him back up.

[Music Cue # 10A: PHANTOM FUGUE PART II]

CHOLET.
PHANTOM!
THE OPERA'S BEEN INVADED BY A PHANTOM!
   LEDOUX.
THE OPERA'S BEEN INVADED BY A PHANTOM!
   CHOLET.   **LEDOUX.**

PHANTOM! THE OPERA'S BEEN INVADED	
BY A GHOST	BY A GHOST
BY A GHOST	BY A GHOST
BY A GHOST	
IF YOU FOLLOW HIM YOU'RE FOLLOWING A PHANTOM	
ENSEMBLE. (*Joins in.*)	
A PHANTOM	
	THE OPERA'S BEEN INVADED BY A PHANTOM
A PHANTOM	
	THE OPERA'S BEEN INVADED BY A PHANTOM
A PHANTOM	
	THE OPERA'S BEEN INVADED BY A GHOST
BY A GHOST	
	BY A GHOST
BY A GHOST	
	BY A GHOST
IF YOU HURRY AND YOU'RE SCURRYING PERHAPS YOU SHOULD BE WORRYING THAT HURRYING AND SCURRYING	

MAY LEAD YOU
    PREMATURELY
TO YOUR END
YOU MAY COME ACROSS
THE PHANTOM.

SEARCH EV'RYWHERE
    AND FIND HIM

                              THE OPERA'S BEEN
                                  INVADED BY A
                                  PHANTOM

SEARCH EV'RYWHERE
    AND FIND HIM

                              THE OPERA'S BEEN
                                  INVADED BY A
                                  PHANTOM

SEARCH EV'RYWHERE
    AND FIND HIM

                              THE OPERA'S BEEN
                                  INVADED BY A GHOST

BY A GHOST, BY A GHOST

BY A GHOST, BY A GHOST

IF YOU FOLLOW HIM
YOU'RE FOLLOWING A
    PHANTOM

                              SEARCH EV'RYWHERE
                                  AND FIND HIM

THE OPERA'S BEEN
    INVADED
BY A PHANTOM

                              SEARCH EV'RYWHERE
                                  AND FIND HIM

THE OPERA'S BEEN
    INVADED
BY A GHOST

                              BY A GHOST, BY A GHOST,

BY A GHOST, BY A GHOST

HE'S A FIEND
HE'S A GHOUL
HE WILL KILL, HE WILL
    RULE
HE WILL MANGLE, HE'LL
    ENTANGLE
HE WILL STRANGLE
    ANYONE
HE DOESN'T CARE
BEWARE ...
THE PHANTOM.

AHHHHH!   PHANTOM
AHHHHH!   PHANTOM
AHHHHH!   PHANTOM
AHHHHH!   PHANTOM
AHHHHH!   PHANTOM
AHHHHH!   PHANTOM
AHHHHH!   PHANTOM

HE WEARS A MASK, A
    MASK
A TERRIFYING MASK,
HE WEARS A MASK
A TERRIFYING MASK!

(Scream!)

SEARCH EV'RYWHERE   PHANTOM!
    AND FIND HIM
                           THE OPERA'S BEEN
                               INVADED BY A
                               PHANTOM

SEARCH EV'RYWHERE
    AND FIND HIM
                           THE OPERA'S BEEN
                               INVADED BY A
                               PHANTOM

SEARCH EV'RYWHERE
  AND FIND HIM

THE OPERA'S BEEN
  INVADED BY A GHOST

BY A GHOST, BY A GHOST

BY A GHOST, BY A GHOST

IF YOU FOLLOW HIM
YOU'RE FOLLOWING A
  PHANTOM

SEARCH EV'RYWHERE
  AND FIND HIM

THE OPERA'S BEEN
  INVADED BY A
  PHANTOM

SEARCH EV'RYWHERE
  AND FIND HIM

THE OPERA'S BEEN
  INVADED BY A
  PHANTOM

SEARCH EV'RYWHERE
  AND FIND HIM

THE OPERA'S BEEN
  INVADED BY A GHOST

BY A GHOST, BY A GHOST,

BY A GHOST, BY A GHOST,

HE'S A FIEND
HE'S A GHOUL
HE WILL KILL, HE WILL
  RULE
HE WILL MANGLE, HE'LL
  ENTANGLE
HE WILL STRANGLE
  ANYONE
HE DOESN'T CARE
BEWARE …

THE ...

PHANTOM!

[Music Cue # 10AA: POST FUGUE]

(LIGHTS OFF down below and UP on the PHANTOM and CHRISTINE in the music room. SHE is standing by the piano. As always, it's NIGHT.
[Music Cue #10B: INTO MUSIC LESSON]
The PHANTOM closes the cover of the keyboard, turns away from her and stares out, overcome with emotion.)

CHRISTINE. ... Have I done something wrong? (*HE shakes his head no.*) My voice doesn't please you!

THE PHANTOM. *Please* me? Ever since I was a child, you are what I've been hearing in my dreams. (*Rising.*) ... I can't teach you anymore.

CHRISTINE. (*Scared.*) What do you *mean*?

THE PHANTOM. I mean, you are ready.

CHRISTINE. ... Ready for what?

THE PHANTOM. To audition for the company.

CHRISTINE. ... Oh, but they're not holding auditions anymore.

THE PHANTOM. You're not going to audition in the usual way. Madam Carlotta would be much too jealous of your voice! No, you will audition at *the Bistro*.

CHRISTINE. ... The Bistro?

THE PHANTOM. Yes. Just across the Place de l'Opera. It's where the Company goes. At the Bistro, everybody sings. It's the custom. It's why they love going there. At the proper moment you will sing there too. Then *everyone* will hear. And there'll be no way La Carlotta can say no. *I even know what you will wear.* Yes, we wait for the proper moment.

CHRISTINE. It's like a dream!

[Music Cue # 11: YOU ARE MUSIC]

THE PHANTOM. Except it's real. Sometimes, dreams *can* be real. ... Christine Daeé, the Gods smiled when they imagined you. (*HE sings.*)
DO RE MI FA SOL
FA RE FA MI
DO RE MI FA SOL
FA RE MI DO.
  Now, *you* ...
CHRISTINE.
DO RE ME FA SOL
FA RE FA MI
DO RE MI FA SOL
FA RE MI DO ...
  PHANTOM. Move the "do" ...
  CHRISTINE. (*In another key.*)
DO RE ME FA SOL
FA RE FA MI
DO RE MI FA SOL
FA RE MI DO ...
  BOTH.
DO RE ME FA SOL
FA RE FA MI
DO RE MI FA SOL
FA RE MI DO ...
  THE PHANTOM.
OH, YOU ARE MUSIC, BEAUTIFUL MUSIC
AND YOU ARE LIGHT TO ME.
OH, YOU ARE MUSIC, MOONBEAMS OF MUSIC
AND YOU ARE LIFE TO ME

DO RE MI FA SOL
FA RE FA MI
TAKE A BREATH ON "ONE"
AND AFTER "THREE"...

CHRISTINE.
DO RE MI FA SOL
FA RE FA MI
BREATHING FIRST ON "ONE"
AND AFTER "THREE."
   PHANTOM.
BREATHING IN THE AIR, AN EBB AND FLOW
BREATHING TAKING CARE ... FA RE, MI DO.
   BOTH.
BREATHING OUT THE AIR FROM DEEP BELOW
READY FOR THE RUN FROM DO TO DO......

OH, YOU ARE MUSIC, BEAUTIFUL MUSIC,
AND YOU ARE LIGHT TO ME.

OH, YOU ARE MUSIC, SUNBURST OF MUSIC,
AND YOU ARE LIFE TO ME.

*(LIGHTS fade to black. Instantly a NEW MUSIC takes
   over: bright tempo. [Music Cue #12: BISTRO] Sounds
   of a PARTY. Gaiety. Laughter.*
LIGHTS UP on ...
*THE BISTRO! The place is jammed. Champagne
   everywhere. Utter merriment.*
*The GUESTS are all from the opera company. Among
   them we can see CHOLET and CARLOTTA (with the
   MINISTER OF CULTURE), JEAN-CLAUDE,
   FLORA, FLORENCE and FLEURE, the latter three
   vying for the attentions of the COUNT, whose party
   we begin to gather this is. But the COUNT, though
   graciously greeting those guests who are still arriving,
   seems distracted. The reason will soon become clear.*
*At rise, VARIOUS WAITERS are singing as THEY
   serve.)*

WAITERS.
SING! CAN YOU SING!

CAN YOU SING A LITTLE BALLAD
IN BETWEEN THE SALAD
AND THE TETE-DE-VEAU
IF ONLY WE COULD HEAR A MELODY...

CHANTE! WHAT YOU WANT!
MAKE IT LYRICAL AND VOCAL
POPULAR AND LOCAL
JUDGES, TAKE YOUR PLACES
CHORUS, YOU WILL DO THE HARMONY.
    CHORUS.
HARMONY! AHHH ...
    WAITERS.
TONIGHT, THE COUNT DE CHANDON
IS HOSTING AN ELEGANT AFFAIR
THE CREAM OF MUSICAL PARIS
WILL BE THERE!

*(The BAND plays. The WAITERS serve. CARLOTTA
and CHOLET move through.)*

    CHOLET. (*Sotto voce.*) Hope you're going to sing.
    CARLOTTA. (*Sotto voce.*) Not sure it would be
fair.
    CHOLET. Ohhhhh ...
    CARLOTTA. Well, if you insist.

*(HE breathes a sigh of gratitude, and hugs her with love
and pride. As THEY move off, we see...
The COUNT, searching the room for Christine. FLORA,
FLORENCE and FLEURE rush up and surround
him.)*

    FLORA. Oh Philippe, we've missed you so!
    FLORENCE. It's true! When you're not here,
there's just no one for us to sing for, or dance for!

FLEURE. Really! You must never go away from us this long again!

THE COUNT. I'll see what I can do.

(HE moves off. THEY're stunned.)

FLORA. I've never *seen* him like this!

FLORENCE. I know! Seems so distracted!

THE COUNT. *(Heads for Jean-Claude.)* Jean-Claude!

JEAN-CLAUDE. Monsieur le Count!

THE COUNT. *(With great urgency.)* Where is Christine?

JEAN-CLAUDE. *(Feigning innocence.)* Christine, Christine, ...

THE COUNT. Don't joke! I asked you to make sure that everyone was invited. Well I don't see her here.

JEAN-CLAUDE. This is remarkable! Is it possible that Monsieur le Count is in love?

THE COUNT. *(Protesting too much.)* Don't be ridiculous! I hardly know the girl! How could I be in love? ... So, where is she?

JEAN-CLAUDE. I don't know. But I'm sure she knows about the party. It's all anyone's been talking about for days!

THE COUNT. And her lessons?

JEAN-CLAUDE. ... *Lessons*?

THE COUNT. Yes! How are they going?

JEAN-CLAUDE. ... I'm sorry?

THE COUNT. She was to be given singing lessons. I sent Carriere explicit instructions.

JEAN-CLAUDE. Monsieur Carriere was dismissed just before she came.

THE COUNT. Ah!

JEAN-CLAUDE. She's been put in the costume department.

THE COUNT. ... *Costume* department?

JEAN-CLAUDE. Under the circumstances, it was the best I could do. I'm sorry.

(The COUNT, though thrown by this news, smiles sympathetically and pats JEAN-CLAUDE on the back. HE moves toward FLORENCE who is approaching him with glass in hand.)

FLORENCE. Philippe, I was thinking...

(The COUNT, absent-mindedly takes the glass from her, passes her and drinks its contents.
CARRIERE enters.)

CARRIERE. Philippe!

(The COUNT turns, see Carriere, and again, absent-mindedly hands the glass back to FLORENCE as HE passes her by on his way to Carriere.)

THE COUNT. Gerard! (*THEY hug.*) Jean-Claude has just told me what happened. You didn't deserve this.
CARRIERE. (*With a wry laugh.*) I agree! Well, what does it matter? I should have retired years ago! We both know that. (*Brighter.*) So, where is this girl I've been told you wanted me to meet.
THE COUNT. Well, she's not here! I'm not even sure she's coming Oh Gerard, I tell you she has the most magical voice you've ever heard!
CARRIERE. (*With a warm smile and a nod.*) Like *all* the women you sent to me for lessons.
THE COUNT. No! No-no, *this one's different!*

(CARRIERE laughs and gives Philippe an understanding, playful, fatherly hug.
CHRISTINE enters looking radiant in a glorious white dress.

The moment she is noticed, a BUZZ begins. Apparently, no one is quite sure who it is. It's with good reason: no one has seen Christine looking even remotely like this.
From where the Count is standing, HE can't yet see her. CHRISTINE begins to walk through the throng. As she does, the WHISPERS increase—who is this vision of beauty?)

CARLOTTA. *(To Cholet.)* ... I think I've seen her before!
CHOLET. Yes ...

(The COUNT, hearing the commotion, turns. HE knows who it is.)

THE COUNT. Christine!
FLORA, FLORENCE, FLEURE. *(Together, stunned.) Christine?*

(Instantly the word spreads like wildfire. The chain leads directly to Carlotta.)

CARLOTTA. My *costume* girl?

(CHRISTINE passes Carlotta with a huge smile. CARLOTTA grabs the nearest drink and downs it.)

THE COUNT. *(Rushing over to Christine.)* Christine! Christine! I am so glad you came! *(Drawing her aside.)* My word of honor! I did not intend for this to happen!
CHRISTINE. What?
THE COUNT. Your working in costumes.
CHRISTINE. Oh ... !
THE COUNT. I said you should have lessons and you *shall*!

CHRISTINE. Really, it's all right, monsieur. I'm honored just being *in* the Opera House.
THE COUNT. No! I gave my word. Your voice needs developing. Believe me, I know about these things!
HEAD WAITER. (*To all.*) *Let the contest BEGIN!*

(*The BAND picks up the volume.*)

THE COUNT. (*To Christine.*) Will you sing?
CHRISTINE. If you like.
THE COUNT. I would! Very much! Then *everyone* will hear!
THE WAITERS.
SING! CAN YOU SING!
CAN YOU SING A LITTLE BALLAD
IN BETWEEN THE SALAD
AND THE TETE-DE-VEAU
IF ONLY WE COULD HEAR A MELODY...

CHANTE! WHAT YOU WANT!
MAKE IT LYRICAL AND VOCAL
POPULAR AND LOCAL
JUDGES, TAKE YOUR PLACES
CHORUS, YOU WILL DO THE HARMONY
CHORUS.
HARMONY, AHHHHH!
CARLOTTA. (*To all.*) Tonight?—only songs about Paris! I will begin the competition. (*SHE takes the first turn. Sings.*)
PAREE ... PAREE IS A LARK, A STROLL IN THE
  PARK
A BAGATELLE!
PAREE ... PAREE IS A CHANCE TO FIND, WHILE
  IN FRANCE,
LA VIE PLUS BELLE.

AS CHARMING AND ALMOST AS GORGEOUS AS
  ME
IS PAREE ... IS PAREE!

(CHEERS and SHOUTS of "bravo!")

HEAD WAITER. Who's next?
THE COUNT. CHRISTINE!
CARLOTTA. ... *Christine?*
THE COUNT. Why not?
CARLOTTA. She's my *costume* girl!
THE COUNT. She has a very nice voice! I've heard
it! *(To Christine.)* Go on. Don't be afraid.

(CHRISTINE starts towards the front.
CARLOTTA, indeed everyone, prepares for a debacle.
  Malevolent GIGGLES can be heard. The CROWD is
  abuzz. At the COUNT's urging, CARRIERE moves
  closer to watch; it seems only HE and the COUNT
  expect anything but disaster.
As CHRISTINE moves forward, a mysterious FIGURE
  appears outside the bistro—one can see him through a
  steamy window. It's a MAN in a slouch hat and
  greatcoat, collar up. A scarf is pulled up around his
  face. HE's staring in.
CHRISTINE smiles sweetly at Carlotta and begins to
  sing.)

CHRISTINE.
MELODY MELODY MELODY MELODY
SUNG SO MELODIOUSLY

(To their amazement, the GUESTS instantly realize—she
  can sing!)

CHRISTINE.
MELODY MELODY, MY KIND OF MELODY

GENTLE AND FLOWING AND FREE

(On the other hand, what she's singing reveals nothing of a bravura nature. SHE is certainly no serious challenge to a true opera diva!)

CHRISTINE.
SOARING ABOVE EVERY ROOFTOP
WHISPERING UNDER EACH TREE
MELODY MELODY
MY MELODIE DE PARIS.
    CARLOTTA. *(To some others, with a grudging smile.)* It's a sweet little voice. *Weak, ...* but sweet.

(And with that, CHRISTINE takes off!—up into the vocal stratosphere!)

CHRISTINE.
LA LA LA ... etc.

(Even the COUNT had not expected this. This is bel canto at its finest! Everywhere: utter astonishment. It's as if God had just arrived. CARRIERE seems especially startled.
As for CARLOTTA—SHE looks like she's about to go into cardiac arrest.
CHRISTINE ends with a staggering run leading to the highest, most perfect note since Yma Sumac was in her prime.
Shouts everywhere of "Bravo! Sing more! MORE!" Even FLORA, FLORENCE and FLEURE seem to have been won over.
Members of the COMPANY shout their agreement. CHRISTINE resumes singing.
Poor CARLOTTA!—it's the lowest moment of her life.)

CHRISTINE.
HOLD ME AND LOVE ME AS YOU WOULD LOVE
  PARIS.

SQUEEZE MY KNEE
IN THE TUILERIES
TAKE ME DANS TES BRAS
IN THE BOIS DE BOULOGNE AND

HOLD ME AND KISS ME
AS YOU WOULD KISS PARIS—
MONTPARNASSE, JE T'EMBRASSE
TAKE ME AWAY, ALONS-Y!
    CHRISTINE/TWO TENORS.
ALONG THE RIVER SEINE
CUDDLE AND AMUSE ME
TELL ME THEN
HOW YOU CAME TO CHOOSE ME.
TELL ME WHEN,
IF YOU EVER LOSE ME,
YOU WILL FEEL YOU'VE LOST
PARIS
    CHRISTINE.
ITSELF ALONG WITH ME
    CHRISTINE/TWO TENORS.
AND UNDERNEATH THE STARS
WE'LL CONTINUE WALKING
PAST THE BARS,
NUZZLING AND TALKING,
    CHRISTINE.
WITH THE STARS
STARING DOWN AND GAWKING
AT THE LOVERS SUCH AS WE...
LOVING IN PARIS
LOVING IN PARIS
PARIS! PARIS!
THE FANTASIE IS TOLD ME EVERY TIME YOU

CHRISTINE/TWO TENORS/ENSEMBLE.
HOLD ME AND KISS ME
AS YOU WOULD KISS PARIS,
  CHRISTINE.
GO WITH ME, TOI, JE T'EN PRIE, MOI!
TAKE ME AWAY THERE
AND PROMISE WE'LL STAY THERE,
OH, TAKE ME AWAY...
ALONS-Y!

AH PARIS, AH PARIS, AH PARIS, PARIS, PARIS...!

(CHRISTINE is lifted onto a table and joined in song by
   the COMPANY, now her *company too.)*

COMPANY.	**CHRISTINE.**
MELODY, MELODY,	PARIS
MELODY, MELODY	
SUNG SO	
MELODIOUSLY	
MELODY, MELODY	PARIS
MY KIND OF MELODY	
GENTLE AND	
FLOWING AND FREE	
SOARING ABOVE	
EVERY ROOFTOP	
WHISPERING UNDER	
EACH TREE	
MELODY, MELODY	
MY MELODIE DE PARIS	
MELODY, MELODY	
MY MELODIE DE	
PARIS!	

(Huge CHEERS from all.)

MINISTER OF CULTURE. Cholet! Sign her up!

PATRON. Yes, sign her up!
CHOLET. I am! I am!

(CHOLET rushes to CHRISTINE and gives her a contract to sign.)

OPERA DIVA. (*With no trace of jealousy*.) Can you believe it? Your costume girl has a better voice than any ONE of us?

(CARLOTTA throws a drink in her face. The CHEERING continues.)

THE COUNT. Think what she'll be like when she's had *lessons*.

(CARLOTTA strides over to CHRISTINE, who is still taking bows for her performance.)

CARLOTTA. Brava! Brava! (*To the company*.) Quiet! Quiet! Quiet (*To Christine, when they're quieted*.) My dear, what did my husband sign you up for?
CHRISTINE. I think ... for my voice.
CARLOTTA. (*As if to a ninny*.) I *understand* for your voice! I mean, for what *role*?

(CHOLET shows her the contract.)

CHRISTINE. (*Reads*.) "Chorus."
CARLOTTA. (*With a sneer*.) "Chorus?" (*To Cholet*.) This woman deserves *better*! (*To Christine*.) My dear, you must sing only *leading* roles!

(BUZZING of astonishment everywhere.)

CHRISTINE. But ... I have no *experience*!

CARLOTTA. You have "TALENT!" (*To Cholet, grandly.*) I want this woman to sing ... Titania.
VARIOUS MEMBERS OF THE COMPANY. (*In astonishment.*) Titania ... !!!?
CHRISTINE. In *The Fairy Queen*?
CARLOTTA. Good. You know the repertoire. (*To everyone.*) Yes! In *The Fairy Queen*! (*MURMURS of disbelief from all around.*) No, she can do it. I know she can!
CHRISTINE. Oh my God ...
CARLOTTA. A talent like yours, my dear, it comes along maybe once in a lifetime. It's the least that I can do.

(*CHEERS from the COMPANY for Carlotta's generosity. SHE smiles with gratitude, turns and strides off with a flourish, like a matador after the kill.*
The COUNT rushes up to CHRISTINE, who is in shock.)

THE COUNT. You know what? I don't think you need lessons at ALL!
CHRISTINE. (*Hugging him.*) Oh Philippe!
THE COUNT. (*Gesturing for Carriere to come over.*) Gerard! Gerard!

(*CARRIERE comes over.*)

THE COUNT. Christine, this is my dear friend, Gerard Carriere.
CHRISTINE. Oh yes!—the man I was supposed to see!
THE COUNT. (*To Carriere.*) Did I tell you she was wonderful? I did! I knew it!
CARRIERE. Mademoiselle, not only is your voice astonishing in and of itself, for me it is astonishing in even *more* ways. For it reminded me of someone I was

privileged to know many years ago—a great singer—
Belladova, I'm sure you never heard of her.
CHRISTINE. No.
CARRIERE. Well, ... no matter. (*To them both.*)
Go. Enjoy your success.

[Music Cue #12A: COUNT/CHRISTINE]

(*The COUNT takes Christine's hand. HE leans close and
whispers something. SHE nods excitedly. MUSIC
under.*
*The LIGHTS BEGIN TO FADE on everyone but the
COUNT and CHRISTINE, heading for the door.
EVERYONE else has frozen in space. It's as if only
Christine and the Count exist at this moment. They ...*
*... and ANOTHER MAN, for as they pass a window we
can see the MAN in the greatcoat staring in, watching
them. There's just enough light to see, above his scarf,
a mask!*
*The walls of the bistro fly away. All the REVELERS
disappear into the shadows. The PHANTOM watches
as CHRISTINE and the COUNT run off, like lovers.*
*One dark CHORD is heard—an echo of the Phantom's
sudden despair.*
*The scene shifts. The PHANTOM staring after Christine
is the last image we see of this one.*
*In the dark, a new MUSIC is heard—as romantic, bright,
and bubbly as champagne. LIGHTS UP on the
Avenue de l'Opera. A MOON glows behind the Opera
House's dome. We can even see the BISTRO, lit in the
distance.*
*The COUNT and CHRISTINE come forward. HE has a
bottle of champagne and two glasses. As HE starts to
uncork the bottle, SHE points to its label.*)

CHRISTINE. This has your name on it.

THE COUNT. (*Embarrassed.*) Yes ... Well! ... (*Modestly, as HE pops it open.*) ... It was the best I could find. (*HE pours her a glass.*) Actually, I feel foolish giving you champagne at all.

CHRISTINE. Why?

THE COUNT. How does one give champagne to champagne?

CHRISTINE. (*Laughing.*) Oh, monsieur! I was not that good.

[Music Cue #13: WHO COULD EVER HAVE
DREAMED UP YOU?]

THE COUNT. "Not that good?" Christine ...! (*HE sings.*)
YOU WERE THE BEST, YOU WIN THE PRIZE
YOU MADE THE NIGHT EFFERVESCENT.
THE DRESS, THE VOICE, THE LOWS, THE HIGHS
IT WAS BEYOND INCANDESCENT!

CAN IT HAVE BEEN I WHO FIRST FOUND YOU?
CAN THESE BE MY ARMS NOW AROUND YOU?
SUCH POETRY!
CAN YOU BE REAL?
OR ARE YOU SOMEONE IMAGINED?

WHO COULD EVER HAVE DREAMED UP YOU?
WHAT KIND OF MIND
COULD EVER HAVE MADE THAT FACE?
THERE COULDN'T BE TWO
IN HEAVEN AND EARTH LIKE YOU
ONE OF A KIND, LIKE HOLDING TWO PAIR OF
   ACES
I WAS NOTHING AND NOWHERE TILL NOW
BUT FROM THIS MOMENT I'LL ONLY GO WHERE
YOU GO!
I HOPE HE'S TAKING A BOW

WHOEVER KNEW WHAT TO DO,
THAT SOMEONE WONDERFUL WHO ONCE
DREAMED UP YOU.

OH, CHRISTINE. I'M IN LOVE WITH YOU!
TOTALLY GONE, DEFEATED AND ALL ASKEW!
I'M FEELING IT START
A CRAZINESS OVER YOU

LEAD THE WAY ON, NO MATTER TO WHERE, I'LL
  FOLLOW!
LOVE COMPLETELY ADORING AND NEW
CAN YOU BELIEVE I FEEL MYSELF SOARING
IT'S TRUE—I LOVE YOU!
  (*Speaks*.) And from the first moment I saw you! It's
really true! *C'est vrai! Absolutement!*
  CHRISTINE. (*Sings*.)
TELL ME ONCE AGAIN, TELL ME ONCE AGAIN
ON A SCALE OF TEN
WAS I MAYBE SIX OR SEVEN?
  THE COUNT.
MORE!
  CHRISTINE.
DON'T EXAGGERATE
SEVEN-AND-A-HALF OR EIGHT
ANY MORE THAN THAT I'D
BE IN HEAVEN...

THE COUNT.	CHRISTINE.
OH, CHRISTINE I'M IN LOVE WITH YOU.	CAN IT EVEN BE? DID I HIT THE "G"?
I'M GONE ...	DID LEARN THE TRILL? NEVER MIND I WILL...
AND ALL ASKEW, A LOVE...	WAS I REALLY GOOD?

ADORING...AND   DID I MOVE THE WAY I
  NEW...   SHOULD?

CAN YOU BELIEVE I
  FEEL MYSELF
  SOARING?
IT'S TRUE, I LOVE
  YOU!
   CHRISTINE.
PHILIPPE, PLEASE WAIT JUST A MOMENT...
THE WORDS YOU SAY, THE THINGS I FEEL
ARE GETTING A BIT CONFUSING.
SOME THINGS YOU KNOW, SOME THINGS YOU
  DON'T
IT COMPLICATES WHAT I'M CHOOSING
SO MUCH TO ABSORB AND TO PONDER
MY HEART, JUST AS YOURS, GROWING
  FONDER...
I HATE TO SPEAK—PERHAPS NEXT WEEK
I'LL COME TO AN UNDERSTANDING...

WHO WOULD EVER HAVE DREAMED OF THIS...
  THAT I'D BE HERE
WITH SOMEONE I'D LOVE TO KISS
IT'S SOMETHING SO PURE IT ALMOST
  APPROACHES BLISS!
THE KIND OF GIFT THAT COMES TO SO VERY
  FEW...
   BOTH.
OH SOMEONE WONDERFUL ... MUST HAVE
  DREAMED UP
YOU!

*(FADE to BLACK. [Music Cue #13A: DRESSING FOR
THE NIGHT] LIGHTS lift. We're outside the Opera.
Time has passed. FIRST NIGHTERS are arriving.
SANDWICH-BOARD MEN carry placards*

announcing The Fairy Queen *and MUSIC: DRESSING FOR THE NIGHT—Reprise.)*

FIRST NIGHTER #1. (*With orchestra under.*) Tickets? Anyone have any extra tickets?

(Tacit.)

FIRST NIGHTER #2. I hear the Count de Chandon discovered her.
FIRST NIGHTER #3. On a street.
FIRST NIGHTER #4. On a street?
FIRST NIGHTER #5. On a street!

(MUSIC continues.)

FIRST NIGHTER #1. (*With orchestra under.*) Tickets? Anyone have any extra tickets?

(Tacit.)

FIRST NIGHTER #5. They say she's never been on a stage before.
FIRST NIGHTER #6. And she's singing "Titania"?

(MUSIC continues.)

FIRST NIGHTER #1. (*With orchestra under.*) Tickets? Anyone have any extra tickets?

(Tacit.)

FIRST NIGHTER #7. At rehearsal last week, the word is, she was extraordinary.
FIRST NIGHTER #8. They've never heard "Titania" sung better.

FIRST NIGHTER #9. How astonishing!

(MUSIC continues.)

FIRST NIGHTER #1. *(With orchestra under.)* Tickets? Anyone have any extra tickets?

(Tacit.)

FIRST NIGHTER #10. I hear La Carlotta is her biggest fan.
FIRST NIGHTER #11. La Carlotta? Unbelievable!

(MUSIC continues. As last PERSON and SANDWICH-BOARD MAN exit, the LIGHTS cross-fade to Christine's dressing room.
CHRISTINE, dressed as Titania, is at her dressing table. The PHANTOM is with her. SHE fumbles with a few strands of her hair.)

CHRISTINE. God, I'm so nervous!
THE PHANTOM. Don't be. You're going to be wonderful. As wonderful as anyone has ever seen or heard ... or dreamed

(A KNOCK on her door.)

CHRISTINE. One moment.

(The PHANTOM exits through a secret panel.)

THE PHANTOM. Till later...

(The panel that slides shut is a full length mirror.)

CHRISTINE. *(Nervously.)* Yes. Come in.

(PHILIPPE enters.)

CHRISTINE. Philippe!

(HE walks towards her, one hand behind his back.)

CHRISTINE. Oh, Philippe, is this really happening?
THE COUNT. Of course it is. And I'm not surprised either. I've always known how exceptional you are. Now everybody else will know.

(HE holds out a rose. SHE takes it, smells its fragrance and clutches it to her. HE kisses her.
Through the mirror, we can detect the outline of the PHANTOM watching.
[Music Cue #13AA: EVERYBODY WILL KNOW]
The LIGHTS cross-fade, revealing ...
Carlotta's dressing room. CARLOTTA is busy mixing some kind of drink in a baronial goblet. The ingredients come from various apothecary jars and vials.
[Music Cue # 13B: THIS PLACE IS MINE—Reprise])

CARLOTTA. *(Sings.)*
OH A DIVA'S WORK IS NEVER DONE...
NO RELIEF, NO TIME FOR FUN ...
(SHE mixes the ingredients into the goblet. Nothing happens.)
NOT IF THE DIVA HAS TO RUN
AN OPERA COMPANY!
(SHE dumps in another; nothing.)
EVERY SMALL DETAIL TO SUPERVISE
EVERY PRETTY FACE TO SCRU--------TINIZE
(SHE takes a vial from her bosom and empties its contents into goblet.)

I PLAN BENEATH THESE EYES THIS OPERA
COMPANY!

(The goblet begins to SMOKE. A KNOCK is heard.)

CARLOTTA. *(Nervously.)* Who is it?
CHOLET. It's me!
CARLOTTA. Just a moment, liebchen! *(SHE
stashes the goblet out of sight.)* Entree!
CHOLET. *(Enters and sniffs the air—something odd;
HE can't tell what.)* Opening night!

*(CHOLET and CARLOTTA go through a ritual of
spitting past each other and then turning around and
bumping rear ends.)*

CHOLET/CARLOTTA. Toie! Toie! Toie!
CARLOTTA. Thought I'd drop in on Christine.
Wish her luck. *(SHE takes the goblet and exits.)*
CHOLET. Of course. *(HE exits.)*

[Music Cue #13C: POISON PATH]

*(LIGHTS cross-fade back to Christine's dressing room.
CARLOTTA knocks on her door.)*

CHRISTINE. Who is it?
CARLOTTA. *(Sweetly.)* Carlotta.
CHRISTINE. Come in.
CARLOTTA. *(Entering.)* Just wanted to wish you
well.
CHRISTINE. I can't believe this is all really
happening!
CARLOTTA. Oh, it is ... Very much.
CHRISTINE. You've been so generous!
CARLOTTA. *(Gaily.)* Nonsense! Opera is my life!
And you, my dear, have one of the sweetest voices I've

ever heard. Believe me, in such a situation, no diva would do any less than I. (*SHE takes the goblet and sips or at least,* seems *to. With relish.*) ... Ahhh! (*SHE puts the goblet down and smiles at Christine.*)

CHRISTINE. What is that?

CARLOTTA. (*Merrily.*) Oh, just a little something made of herbs. Most opera singers use it before going on. Helps steady those nerves! *I'm so nervous!* How you do tonight affects my reputation as well as yours.

CHRISTINE. Please!

CARLOTTA. Oh I'm sorry. I didn't mean to worry you. You're going to do just *splendidly.* I'm convinced of it. (*Lifting the goblet again.*) I'm so nervous for you, without this I don't think I'd even be able to *talk!* (*SHE laughs and takes another sip—or seems to. CHRISTINE stares at her.*) Ahhhhhhh! (*SHE puts the goblet back down, but this time, closer to Christine.*)

JEAN-CLAUDE. (*Voice through door.*) Five minutes.

CHRISTINE. Could I have some?

CARLOTTA. Why? Are you nervous, too?

(CHRISTINE holds out two trembling hands.)

CARLOTTA. Well, then it would probably do you good.

(SHE holds the goblet out. CHRISTINE takes it. SHE takes a sip. Hesitates. Then finishes it.)

CARLOTTA. You know what I can't understand?

CHRISTINE. What?

CARLOTTA. How you learned to sing so well. (*CHRISTINE tenses.*) Because technique like yours simply does not come *on its own.* (*A beat.*) So, who has been training you?

CHRISTINE. ... I can't say.

CARLOTTA. Can't *say*!?

CHRISTINE. *I gave my word.*

CARLOTTA. To whom? Your *teacher*?

CHRISTINE. (*Barely audible.*) Yes.

CARLOTTA. I see! Your teacher said, "Don't tell Carlotta who I am."

CHRISTINE. He said not to tell *anyone*.

CARLOTTA. I'm *anyone*?

CHRISTINE. Madame, *please*!

CARLOTTA. So this is how you repay my generosity.

CHRISTINE. No, no—

CARLOTTA. I've a good mind to set you packing! How DARE you treat me like this!? I've never *heard* of such behavior!

CHRISTINE. All right! The last thing I would want is to appear ungrateful.

CARLOTTA. I would hope.

CHRISTINE. But you must swear never to tell another soul.

CARLOTTA. You have my word!

CHRISTINE. The truth is, I don't *know* what his name is. The maestro has never told me.

CARLOTTA. (*Taken aback.*) Well, ... what does he look like?

CHRISTINE. I don't know that either.

(*CARLOTTA stares back, puzzled.*)

CHRISTINE. ... I've never seen his face.

CARLOTTA. Dear, I'm afraid I don't understand. What does he do, teach you in the dark?

CHRISTINE. He wears a mask.

CARLOTTA. (*Stares at Christine, stunned. Barely audible.*) ... A *mask*!

(*CHRISTINE nods.*)

JEAN-CLAUDE. Company to the stage!

[Music Cue #13D: ORCHESTRA TUNING UP]

(ORCHESTRA begins tuning up.)

CARLOTTA. *(Trying to contain her emotions.)* I'd better go.

(SHE exits the door. CHRISTINE stares into the full length mirror, trying hard not to cry.)

CHRISTINE. *(Softly.)* Maestro, forgive me.

(LIGHTS to black on Christine's dressing room and up on CHOLET next to the pinrail. CARLOTTA rushes over to Cholet.)

JEAN-CLAUDE. Heads up! Scenery coming in! Heads up!
   CARLOTTA. Get Ledoux! We need men with guns! Hurry!
   CHOLET. ... Why?
   CARLOTTA. Guess who her teacher is!?
   JEAN-CLAUDE. Quiet backstage! Curtain going up, curtain going up!

[Music Cue #14: TITANIA]

ENSEMBLE.
HERE COMES TITANIA, HERE COMES TITANIA
THE GREAT TITANIA COMES THIS WAY
THE QUEEN OF FAERIES
ON LITTLE FOOTSTEPS
ON LITTLE FOOTSTEPS
COMES TODAY.

SHE COMES, SHE COMES, TITANIA COMES!
MAKE WAY! MAKE WAY!
HAIL! NOBLE OBERON!
  OBERON.
HAIL, GENTLE FAERIES ALL!
TITANIA, I PRESENT TO YOU
THESE CREATURES OF THE NIGHT.
  TITANIA.
GOOD FAERIES, GENTLE ELVES, GATHER
  ROUND,
MAKE MERRY IN MY SIGHT.

DEAR OBERON, GOOD OBERON,
SWEET OBERON,
(Her VOICE cracks.)

  AUDIENCE. Boo! Boo! *(Etc.)*
  CHOLET. What's happened?
  CARLOTTA. She's gone dry!
  CHOLET. ... But why?
  CARLOTTA. Panic! No experience!

*(ORCHESTRA CONDUCTOR taps her baton on music
  stand.)*

  TITANIA.
DEAR OBERON, GOOD OBERON, SWEET OBERON!
(Her VOICE cracks again.)
  CARLOTTA. I knew you shouldn't have hired her!
You brought this on.

*(The booing and catcalls are now overwhelming. Things
  are being thrown at Christine from the Opera House
  audience. CHRISTINE is too stunned to move.
The COUNT rushes on.)*

[Music Cue # 14A: CHASE I]

THE COUNT. For God sakes, somebody bring down the curtain! My God, they're throwing things at her! (*The COUNT runs out onto the stage.*)

CHOLET. What the hell's he doing out there?

COMPANY MEMBER. Trying to get her off stage! SOMEONE HELP HIM!!

CARRIERE. (*Enters.*) BRING DOWN THE CURTAIN! WHO THE HELL'S IN CHARGE OF THE CURTAIN!?

(*Suddenly the PHANTOM runs through and cuts a rope with a sword cane. The CURTAIN drops to the stage.*)

THE PHANTOM. Christine!
CHOLET. Get him! Get him!
CARRIERE. NO!
CHRISTINE. (*To the Phantom.*) Forgive me!

(*LEDOUX blows his police WHISTLE.*)

CHOLET. Shoot him! Shoot him!
CARRIERE. NO!
CHRISTINE. Oh, my God.

(*THE CHANDELIER falls to the stage in slow motion! Under it are some POLICE, who SCREAM.*

THE CHANDELIER explodes in slow motion. LIGHTS flash like fireworks. More SCREAMS. The fallen chandelier shorts the electricity and the stage goes DARK.

In the dark, PEOPLE scream for the lights. Then we begin to see SHADOWS—people groping about in the dimmest of ambient light. In this light we see CHRISTINE wandering about, lost.

*A recognizable shadow—the PHANTOM!—swoops
down and scoops her off and exits.*
Continued SHOUTS in the dark. It's chaos on the stage!
*LIGHTS UP on Christine's dressing room. The
PHANTOM enters with CHRISTINE. HE locks the
door.)*

THE COUNT'S VOICE. (*From a distance.*)
Christine! Christine ...! (*Calling for help.*) This way!
Over this way! Hurry! Down here! HE'S GOT HER!

*(OTHER VOICES can be heard calling back, in response:
"This way!/Down here!/He's down here!" etc.)*
*During this, the PHANTOM finds Carlotta's goblet,
picks it up and sniffs: something is odd here.*
*The PHANTOM dips a finger into the goblet and tastes
his fingertip.)*

THE PHANTOM. ... Did you drink from this?
CHRISTINE. Yes. Carlotta gave it to me. Why?

(Screaming with fury, The PHANTOM flings it down.)

CHRISTINE. I've let you down!
THE PHANTOM. This was not your fault.

*(Out in the hall, the COUNT runs with OTHERS towards
her dressing room.)*

THE COUNT. (*From the hallway.*) Christine! It's
Philippe!
CHRISTINE. Philippe!

*(SHE faints. The PHANTOM scoops her up into his
arms and heads for his secret panel.)*

THE COUNT. Are you all right? Please let me in! Christine!

(The PHANTOM goes through the opening with Christine, the mirror sliding shut just as the COUNT pushes the door down and rushes in, shouting as he does...)

THE COUNT. Christine! (*Scanning the empty room in amazement.*) ... Christine?

(Christine's dressing room disappears revealing ...
... a secret corridor behind the dressing room. TORCHES illumine a staircase down. Dim sound of the COUNT calling Christine's name; his voice sounds miles away.
The PHANTOM, holding Christine in his arms, descends the staircase.
As the PHANTOM descends, way below, a lagoon with a dark narrow boat tied to a dock moves into view. In the distance is an endless vaulted space. MIST rises from the water. MUSIC.)

[Music Cue #14B: FINAL ACT I]

THE PHANTOM. (*Sings.*)
FIND IN THE WORLD
THIS MIRAGE THAT I SEE
AND FROM THE WORLD
YOU WILL BRING HER TO ME
AND I'LL MAKE HER MINE!

(SLOW CURTAIN)

[Music Cue #15: ENTR'ACTE]

ACT II

[Music Cue # 16: WITHOUT YOUR MUSIC]

Slow curtain up.
We are in the Phantom's domain now. The PHANTOM, standing in the rear of his boat, poles it smoothly through the lagoon. CHRISTINE, lying in the middle of the boat, one arm dangling in the water, is asleep. Shafts of MOONLIGHT beam down through grates high above onto the water.
As the boat glides along, the PHANTOM sings.)

THE PHANTOM.
HERE YOU'LL BE SAFE
FROM THEIR PRYING AND VICIOUS EYES
FAR FROM ALL VENOMOUS WORDS
AND MALICIOUS LIES.

SLEEP GENTLE CREATURE
MY LOVE AND MY PROTEGE
AS FOR MYSELF, I WILL WORSHIP YOU NIGHT
  AND DAY.

(As the boat glides, the set changes. The PHANTOM is approaching a docking area. Along the shore, TORCHES are lit. A magic kingdom begins to unfold—a fairyland of old opera sets. There's even the hint of a castle. His ACOLYTES make ready to secure the boat.)

THE PHANTOM.
ALL MY EXISTENCE WILL END
IF YOU GO AWAY...

77

(An ACOLYTE at the front of the boat lashes it to the dock.)

THE PHANTOM.
LIFE WITHOUT YOUR MUSIC
WOULD BE NOT WORTH LIVING
I'D BE USELESS AS A BELL THAT CANNOT RING
LEFT HERE ALL ALONE
I'D BE A SAD ABANDONED KING
WITHOUT A LAND TO LIVE FOR...

(The PHANTOM lifts Christine into his arms and carries her from the boat onto the shore.)

THE PHANTOM.
LIFE WITHOUT YOUR SWEETNESS
BLEAK, DEAD, INCOMPLETE
A SEASON SILENT AS A BIRD THAT DOESN'T
  SING
ENDLESS, FROZEN TIME
THAT ONLY YOU CAN TURN TO SPRING.

(HE carries her inside his castle—a castle built of opera flats.)

WITHOUT YOUR SPELL
LIKE A MUSICAL CHORD
RUNNING DEEP IN MY MIND
LIKE A SWELL IN A CLASSICAL SYMPHONY,
I AM UNDONE, OUT OF STEP, OUT OF TUNE
I'M A MAN WHO'S GONE BLIND
BROKEN INSIDE
POORLY DESIGNED... AND SO YOU

(CANDELABRA, held by ACOLYTES, burst into light. HE has entered Christine's room! On the wall is a portrait of a woman in a white dress.

*The PHANTOM carries Christine toward a four-poster
    bed with gauzy canopy. HE places her gently on the
    bed. The ACOLYTES withdraw.
HE pulls up the white comforter, singing as he does.)*

THE PHANTOM.
SEE, WITH ALL YOUR MUSIC
ME, WITH ALL YOUR MUSIC
WE'D BE LIKE A RACE APART—
AND NOW YOU'RE HERE
AND WE MAY START.

*(HE puts his hand just above her head. Hesitates. Then,
    ever-so-cautiously, HE strokes her hair. Then, just as
    cautiously, HE kisses her forehead.
And then HE rises and looks up. His expression turns
    somber: a new task is at hand. The MUSIC turns dark.
    [Music Cue #16A: FATHER/SON CONFRONTA-
    TION] HE stalks out of the room with a purposeful
    stride. The LIGHT on the bedroom fades.
CARRIERE emerges from the shadows ahead of him.
    The PHANTOM stops short.)*

THE PHANTOM. (*Cold fury.*) What are you doing
here?
CARRIERE. What do you think?
THE PHANTOM. No one comes down here that I
don't invite!
CARRIERE. *They will not let you get away with
this!*
THE PHANTOM. Well, they may have no choice.
Now get out. I have things to do.
CARRIERE. I want you to send her back!
THE PHANTOM. No! How can you even suggest
such a thing? The world up there is not fit for her! Up
there is where hell is! I will not send an angel to hell.
CARRIERE. Erik—

THE PHANTOM. NO! She was betrayed tonight. And I'd sooner die than let her be betrayed again!

CARRIERE. ... How was she betrayed?

THE PHANTOM. You think she sang like that from nerves? That Carlotta woman poisoned her.

CARRIERE. Oh God.

THE PHANTOM. And you are responsible! This company was in your trust! And you've given it to people who care nothing for beauty.

CARRIERE. You *know* I had no choice.

THE PHANTOM. Of course you did. You could have burned this place down! Better in ashes and memory than this. *Send her back?*

CARRIERE. *Yes*!

THE PHANTOM. Never! I may be hideous, but I am not hideous enough to do that.

CARRIERE. Then they will come down here with dogs and guns and bring her back themselves! Erik, I can't protect you anymore!

THE PHANTOM. It's *they* who'll need protecting here, not I.

CARRIERE. ... What do you mean?

THE PHANTOM. I mean, one push on a certain lever, and the opera season is gone *forever*.

CARRIERE. Erik!

THE PHANTOM. I have lived my entire life in a tomb. Why should I fear one now?

CARRIERE. But she'll die too!

THE PHANTOM. And to a better place she'll quickly go.

CARRIERE. You're sure of that.

THE PHANTOM. Oh I am, I am indeed! Do you suppose I could have lived this long like a dog without knowing *that*?

(CARRIERE starts to protest. ERIK cuts him off.)

THE PHANTOM. *Listen to me*! For as long as I can remember, I have dreamed of her ... People are born for many things, Gerard. I was born to live down here, but till now, I have never known quite why ... I was born *so she could come and save me*! For that is what she's done. She is the *reason* I was born! ... I don't want you to ever come back here again. From now on, she will be all I need. (*Cold tone; distant.*) But I thank you for all you've done for me in the past.

(*CARRIERE goes to the stairs and starts to ascend. Music Cue #16B: WHERE IN THE WORLD— Reprise]*)

THE PHANTOM. (*Sings.*)
WHERE IN THE WORLD, IN THIS MISERABLE
  WORLD
IS A RESPITE FOR ME?
FROM AN AGE THAT THEY KEEP
EVER TAWDRY AND CHEAP
WILL I EVER BREAK FREE?
FREE FROM THE WORLD UP THERE?

(*His ACOLYTES emerge with a selection of masks for him to look over.*)

THE PHANTOM.
HOW THEY ALL GLADLY DESTROY HER BEAUTY!
HEARTLESSLY HOW THEY ABUSE HER CHARM
OH, THEY MUST FEEL THEY ARE SAFE FROM
VENGEANCE
ONE AS WEAK AS SHE COULD DO NO HARM ...

THERE IN THE WORLD, I WILL GO IN THE
WORLD
AND I'LL SEEK OUT THE ONE
WHO WOULD STAMP ON A FLOW'R

WITH UNSPEARABLE POW'R
AND, BEFORE I AM DONE
THIS DAY
THOSE IN THE WORLD WHO WOULD KILL WHAT
IS FINE
THEM I WILL SEEK AND, BY ALL THAT'S DIVINE,

I WILL MAKE THEM PAY!

*(HE chooses a death's head mask, puts it on and exits.
   LIGHTS to black on the ACOLYTES.*
*CARRIERE, who we now see has not ascended all the
   way, but has hidden in the shadows of the stairs,
   reappears.*
HE scans the area.
*LIGHTS UP on Christine's bedroom. MUSIC under.
   [Music Cue #16C: CARRIERE, CHRISTINE] Very
   dreamy, very sweet. The curtains billow.
   MOONLIGHT streams in.*
SHE gets up. SHE looks about in astonishment.
*SHE sees the portrait. It is the portrait of a lovely woman
   in a white dress. The woman resembles Christine.*
CHRISTINE stares at the portrait.
CARRIERE makes his way to her room.
Sensing his presence, SHE turns.)

CHRISTINE. ... Maestro?
CARRIERE. No. But he'll be back soon, so you
must get out at once. (*HE moves towards her. The
SHADOWS still obscure his face.*)
CHRISTINE. Who are you?
CARRIERE. A friend. (*Emerging into the light.*) ...
Gerard Carriere. We met at the bistro.
CHRISTINE. (*Seeing him now.*) Oh yes! Of
course. You said my voice reminded you of a certain
singer.

CARRIERE. That's right. Unfortunately, it's reminded someone else of her as well. Which is why you're in great danger. Come. I know the way.

(HE takes her hand. SHE pulls away.)

CHRISTINE. No! Wait. Please! ... *Where am I*?
CARRIERE. In the catacombs underneath the opera house.
CHRISTINE. This is all a dream ...
CARRIERE. Mademoiselle, believe me, for your life depends on it, *you are not dreaming.* Erik brought you down.
CHRISTINE. ... Erik?
CARRIERE. Your maestro. Most people know him as the Phantom of the Opera.
CHRISTINE. I don't believe this!
CARRIERE. You had better. Unless you wish to stay down here with him forever. Because I believe that's what he's planning.
CHRISTINE. *What*!?
CARRIERE. He's in love with you, I'm sure of it. He *has* to be. And he has *always* been. That woman whose voice I said yours reminded me of? She was his mother. That's her portrait.
CHRISTINE. What *is* this place?
CARRIERE. This is where Erik lives.
CHRISTINE. Oh my God ... (*A beat.*) *Why*?
CARRIERE. Why does he wear a mask?
CHRISTINE. He won't say. Only that I'll never see him with it off.
CARRIERE. For which you should be grateful. If you saw, you'd know why he's lived down here. *Erik doesn't understand your world.* You must get out at once.
CHRISTINE. No. No, I don't care *what* his face looks like. I've seen his eyes, I've heard his voice. There is *kindness* inside of him.

CARRIERE. Of course. And there has always been. But his face is like death. And to know him, you must also know his face ... Get out of here while you still can. Erik cannot be helped by anyone.

CHRISTINE. How do you know all this?

CARRIERE. (*With great difficulty.*) Because ... I am his father.

[Music Cue #17: STORY OF ERIK PART I]

CARRIERE. His mother was the most perfectly exquisite woman I'd ever seen.

(A group of young BALLERINAS dance out and begin practicing at a barre.)

CARRIERE. She was already in the company when I arrived, but as a dancer, not a singer. No one knew yet that she sang.

(This memory takes shape behind them. After awhile, these memories will begin to happen all around.)

CARRIERE. It was a time of great singing. The Opera House had just been completed.

(A young man—YOUNG CARRIERE—enters the class carrying manuscripts. HE heads for the ballet master, eyes on the most beautiful of the dancers, BELLADOVA; SHE bears a marked resemblance to Christine.)

CARRIERE. I was eighteen, and had come as an apprentice to the manager.

(As BELLADOVA dances past him, their eyes meet. That moment "freezes." The dancers exit, leaving BELLADOVA and YOUNG CARRIERE.
The MUSIC shifts to a "Love Interlude"—YOUNG CARRIERE and BELLADOVA fall in love and become lovers.)

CARRIERE. We lived only for the moment and our passion swept us away. (*A pause.*) Why me? ... She could have had anyone. Why was it me?

(We can dimly make out BELLADOVA lying with YOUNG CARRIERE in what seems to be a field of grass by a stream. Lovely, late AFTERNOON LIGHT.)

CARRIERE. I asked her once. We were by a stream I think. A warm, autumn day ...

CARRIERE AND YOUNG CARRIERE. (*Together. YOUNG CARRIERE's voice echoing.*) Why on earth do you love *me*?

(BELLADOVA laughs.)

CARRIERE. And then something happened, so astonishing, it made me wonder more about the wonder of her than her unlikely love for me ... *She sang!*

(BELLADOVA begins to sing. No lyrics, just the word "la" repeated. YOUNG CARRIERE sits upright, startled. Her voice is glorious and sounds quite like Christine's.)

BELLADOVA.
LA LA LA LA LA
LA LA LA LA LA LA LA LA

LA LA LA LA LA LA LA LA
LA LA LA LA LA LA
LA LA ...
    CARRIERE. (*HE sings.*)
NEVER BEFORE HAD A VOICE
LIKE THAT VOICE
EVER BEEN ON A STAGE
    BELLADOVA.
LA LA ...
    CARRIERE.
OH, IT WAS MORE THAN A VOICE
IT BELONGED TO THE WORLD
IT BELONGED TO THE AGE.
    BELLADOVA.
LA LA LA LA LA
LA LA LA LA LA LA LA LA
LA LA LA LA LA LA LA LA
LA LA LA LA LA LA
LA LA ...
    CARRIERE. (*HE speaks.*) It was a voice of absolute transparency and warmth. It was utter beauty! I'd had no idea she could sing at all! ... No one knew. (*A beat.*) At my urging, she auditioned for the Company.
    BELLADOVA.
LA LA...

*(BELLADOVA stands before several stern-faced MEN in
    dark suits. THEY applaud her silently.)*

    CARRIERE. She was hired. And quickly became the toast of Paris. All was perfection! (*A pause; somberly.*) ... And then she said she was bearing my child. And wanted to get married ... Oh God, how I wished I could! But there was something I had not told her: I was already married and she was not prepared for that. She prayed to the Virgin Mary for strength.

(We see BELLADOVA in a church, singing.)

BELLADOVA.
VIERGE MARIE
SAVE ME
BRING MY SALVATION
AVE MARIA
HELP THIS POOR LAMB.
PENITENTS.
AVE, AVE, AVE, AVE MARIA
AVE, AVE, AVE, AVE MARIA
VIERGE MARIE
SAVE ME BRING MY SALVATION
AVE MARIA
HELP THIS POOR LAMB.

*(During the course of the song, a transformation occurs.
BELLADOVA has become hugely pregnant.)*

CARRIERE. But God did not answer her cry ... or
anyway, did not seem to.

(The church scene fades away, as does BELLADOVA.)

CARRIERE. Soon after that, she disappeared. I
searched everywhere for her, but in vain. Some months
later, I saw her buying herbs from a gypsy woman near
Notre Dame. I hardly recognized her.

*(We see BELLADOVA buying powders and herbs from
the gypsy. SHE looks unkempt, and almost deranged.
SHE's also very pregnant. SHE starts to drink the
potion. YOUNG CARRIERE races up to her. HE
struggles to keep her from taking what she's bought.)*

CARRIERE. No! (*But BELLADOVA takes the
potion, despite his struggle. SHE turns to YOUNG*

CARRIERE for help.) She asked me to help her back to where she had been living. It was down here.

(SHE goes into labor. We see YOUNG CARRIERE helping her with the birth. As he does, we hear the CHORUS.)

PENITENTS.
VIERGE MARIE
SAVE ME
BRING MY SALVATION
AVE MARIA
HELP THIS POOR ...

(We hear the sound of a SLAP. Then the SOUND of a BABY CRYING. YOUNG CARRIERE stares down at his new-born son in horror.)

CARRIERE. His face was like nothing I had ever seen. As beautiful as she had been, that's how monstrous Erik was.

[Music Cue #17A: STORY OF ERIK PART II]

(Pause.)

CARRIERE. I think the hardest part for me was realizing that she truly saw nothing ugly in this child at all. To her, he was beauty itself. And to him, ... so was she.
BELLADOVA. *(Sings.)*
FA RE MI DO ...
OH YOU ARE MUSIC
BEAUTIFUL MUSIC
AND YOU ARE LIFE TO ME.

(YOUNG ERIK enters. HE is now about eight. We do not see his face in any kind of light that allows us to see details.)

YOUNG ERIK.
LA LA LA LA LA
LA LA LA LA LA LA LA LA
LA LA LA LA LA
LA LA LA LA LA LA
LA LA
C A R R I E R E . Then one night, she died. *(BELLADOVA exits, eyes on the child as she goes.)* As best I could, I raised him myself. When he was eight, he noticed his reflection in the lagoon.

(YOUNG ERIK kneels and stares down into the water.)

CARRIERE. He thought he had seen a sea monster!
YOUNG ERIK. AGGGGHHH!
CARRIERE. I fashioned him a mask, which made things somewhat easier ... At least, for me.

(YOUNG CARRIERE helps him put on a mask and YOUNG ERIK sings.)

YOUNG ERIK.
VIERGE MARIE SAVE ME
BRING MY SALVATION
AVE MARIA
HELP THIS POOR LAMB.
(YOUNG ERIK covers his face and begins to sob.)
CARRIERE. At night, he would cry, and those cries echoed up through the shafts and cracks. *I was not the only one who could hear!* And thus, the legend of the opera ghost was born.
ALL.
VIERGE MARIE

SAVE ME BRING MY SALVATION
AVE MARIA
HELP THIS POOR LAMB.
AHHHHHHH!

*(EVERYONE exits as LIGHTS cross-fade and we are
back in the Phantom's bedroom.)*

*(Carriere's memory FADES from view.
[Music Cue #17B: AFTER ERIK]
LIGHTS back up on CHRISTINE.)*

CHRISTINE. Did he *know* you were his father?
CARRIERE. No ... He still doesn't. He thinks I'm
some kind of uncle.
CHRISTINE. (*Appalled.*) Why?
CARRIERE. Cowardice ... I've always known that
someday, one way or another, I would have to abandon
him. And I couldn't bear him knowing his father had left
without taking him along. (*Pause.*) Which is what I now
must do. (*HE turns to her.*) And you must, too.
CHRISTINE. No!
CARRIERE. If you wait, he will not let you go at
all!
CHRISTINE. I don't believe that! Especially after
everything you've just said. You want me to leave him
without so much as a *word*? No. He deserves better than
that from me, I think. I will go *when I am ready to ...*
After I have talked with him.
CARRIERE. You are making a terrible mistake!
CHRISTINE. I'm not afraid. I know his heart.
CARRIERE. Unfortunately, there's more to him
than that ... Get out as soon as you can.

[Music Cue #17C: CARLOTTA'S DEMISE]

*(HE turns and leaves. SHE turns and stares at the portrait
of Belladova. The LIGHTS FADE on her room and
COME UP on ... An upper level corridor. The
COUNT, CHOLET, LEDOUX and some POLICE are
striding along.)*

THE COUNT. *(To Ledoux.)* I tell you, she was *in
the dressing room*!
LEDOUX. Did you actually *see* her go in?
THE COUNT. ... I *thought* I did.
LEDOUX. Ahhhh—!
THE COUNT. Oh, for God sakes Ledoux, it's
obvious! That masked fiend has taken her!
LEDOUX. Well, it is not obvious to me!
THE COUNT. Fine! Then I will go down after her
myself!
LEDOUX. Monsieur, if you do, I assure you, you
will not come back alive!

*(The COUNT stares back, startled.
CHOLET moves in next to Ledoux.)*

CHOLET. *(Sotto voce.)* We must keep all this as
quiet as possible.
LEDOUX. I agree.
CHOLET. Not good for business.
LEDOUX. I understand

*(THEY exit. Same for the COUNT.
Suddenly, a voice echoes from all around. It's the
PHANTOM.)*

THE PHANTOM'S VOICE. *(As if beckoning.)*
Carlotta ... Carlotta ...
CARLOTTA. *(Appears from her dressing room and
looks around.)* Who is it?

(The PHANTOM appears, body obscured by the shadows. HE holds a glorious bouquet of flowers.)

THE PHANTOM. Ah! La Carlotta!
CARLOTTA. (*A bit spooked.*) ...Who are you?
THE PHANTOM. An admirer.
CARLOTTA. Ah! (*Moving closer.*) Are those for me?
THE PHANTOM. They are indeed.

(SHE descends.)

THE PHANTOM. I have to say, in all my years, I have never heard a voice quite like yours.
CARLOTTA. (*Coming closer.*) Why, thank you.
THE PHANTOM. Not even in a barnyard.
CARLOTTA. ... (*SHE stops short.*) what?
THE PHANTOM. Where of course I've never been.
CARLOTTA. (*Beginning to realize who it is.*) Oh my God ...
THE PHANTOM. Though I can imagine.

(HE holds out the flowers, revealing his death's head mask. SHE gasps in horror and backs away.)

THE PHANTOM. I present you with a choice. Stay here and die. In which case these flowers are for your grave—a death bouquet! Or leave my Opera House. And I will let you live. In which case, these flowers are a bouquet of forgiveness.
CARLOTTA. *Your* Opera House?
THE PHANTOM. Yes, my Opera House, *indeed* my Opera House! ... And my world.
CARLOTTA. (*With a cold smile.*) Close. (*A beat.*) But, alas, you have it wrong. *You* are the one who is trespassing here. So *you* get out. YOU get out! (*A beat.*) And you can take these flowers with you and use them

for *your* grave! You think I have lived my whole life dreaming of THIS ... just to give it all away?

THE PHANTOM. Then you leave me no choice.

CARLOTTA. No! *You* leave me no choice! HELP!

(The PHANTOM runs off.)

CARLOTTA. HELP! HELP! HE'S OUT HERE! HE'S ON THE STAGE! HELLLLLP! (*SHE starts running up the stairs.*)

(Offstage The PHANTOM pulls a dark cable from the wall. We hear a LOUD CRACKLE and see AN OPEN FLAME and SPARKS FLYING as HE re-enters with a live electric cable.)

THE PHANTOM. What you did to Christine I found almost as shocking as you will find this!

(HE touches the cable to the spiral staircase on which CARLOTTA is rapidly ascending, frantically trying to get away from him. But SHE's not fast enough. The electricity causes explosions and sparks to fly. We hear a loud SIZZLING SOUND. SMOKE rises. SHE is electrocuted. SHE screams.
LIGHTS TO BLACK. In the dark we can still hear CARLOTTA screaming.
LIGHTS UP on THE Phantom's bedroom. CHRISTINE turns, startled as if by a bad dream.
CARLOTTA's scream echoes and fades away.
[Music Cue #17D: WALK IN THE WOODS]
MUSIC under. Very dreamy, very sweet. The curtains billow. MOONLIGHT streams in.
The PHANTOM enters her room, wearing a warm and pleasant mask.
SHE smiles on seeing him.
SILENCE for a moment.

Then ....)

   THE PHANTOM. (*Polite, warm, sweet.*) Did you sleep well?
   CHRISTINE. (*Nervously.*) ... Yes.
   THE PHANTOM. It's a *nice* room, I think. Good, cozy bed. Pleasant water view.
   CHRISTINE. ... Yes.

(Awkward silence.)

   THE PHANTOM. (*Cheerfully.*) Well! What shall we do today? ... I have an idea! How about ... (*Slyly, but good-natured.*) ... a *picnic*?
   CHRISTINE. Picnic?
   THE PHANTOM. Yes ... Through the woods. By the water's edge. And while we stroll, I can show you where I live. My ... (*Proudly.*) ... *domain!* (*HE lifts up a wicker picnic basket.*) Shall we go?

(Much to HER astonishment, the far wall opens. Beyond
   are TREES—two-dimensional, painted opera cut-outs,
   but glorious.
HE gives her his arm. SHE links her arm through his.
   The room slides away.
The PHANTOM and CHRISTINE begin to stroll through
   his mysterious, beautiful opera flat forest. Ahead is a
   clearing, LIGHT shafting through. THEY stroll
   towards the light. As THEY move, the TREES move
   with them, but in an opposite direction—the
   ACOLYTES do it all. BIRD SOUNDS are heard too;
   also made by the acolytes [whom SHE has not yet
   noticed].
SHE is dazzled.)

THE PHANTOM. (*Brightly.*) Do you like these woods of mine? This ancient glade of elms and oak. This wondrous haunt.
CHRISTINE. (*SHE spots the acolytes, moving things. Nervously.*) ... Yes... Very much.

(*Now that she's aware of them, SHE sees them almost everywhere—though THEY are trying to stay out of sight.*)

THE PHANTOM. One can get quite lost in these woods if one doesn't know the path. Or have a guide who does. (*HE smiles at her. The WOODS move past them.*) Once there were only endless, dreary vaults in this land—gloomy barren corridors, a wilderness of stone, no light at all, no love, no loving *kindness.*
CHRISTINE. *Who are those people?*
THE PHANTOM. ... People?
CHRISTINE. (*Pointing.*) There ... And there.
THE PHANTOM. Oh! (*Sotto voce.*) Pay them no heed. They are friends—the faceless of Paris. I allow them access to my park.

(*One of the ACOLYTES makes the sound of a BIRD.*)

THE PHANTOM. Ssh! Sparrow, yes. The morning birds! A dove perhaps. We'll see.

(*THEY resume walking.*)

THE PHANTOM. Pheasants too are here, and deer, and squirrels, geese and rabbits, all playing most harmoniously, like this magic music. You are magic too I think.
CHRISTINE. No ...
THE PHANTOM. Oh you are. I know. Magic cannot hide from me. Magic is my friend. You belong

here ... (*THEY walk on.*) Come, we'll set our picnic here. (*HE spreads the cloth.*) It is, of all the places in my realm, the most enchanted spot I think. (*HE opens the picnic basket.*) Do you like wine?

CHRISTINE. ... Yes.

THE PHANTOM. (*HE pulls out a bottle of wine and two glasses. Nervously.*) Do you like poetry?

CHRISTINE. (*Taken aback.*) ... Yes.

THE PHANTOM. I was sure you did! (*HE lifts a book out of the basket so carefully one would think it both priceless and fragile.*) My favorite poet ... (*HE hands her the book with reverence.*) ... William Blake.

(*SHE stares down at the book.*)

THE PHANTOM. Do you know his work?

(*SHE shakes her head.*)

THE PHANTOM. (*With joy.*) Ahhhh! You have such pleasure ahead! Such *bliss!* (*Pointing to the book.*) That man knows my heart! (*Sotto voce.*) And he has seen God.

(*SHE opens the book and stares down.*)

THE PHANTOM. Know that book, and you know me.

CHRISTINE. (*Reads from a page.*)
"My mother bore me in the southern wild
I live in darkness but my soul is light
Light as the forehead of an English child..."

(*SHE stares up. SHE cannot bring herself to read the next line aloud. HE stares back.*)

THE PHANTOM. (*From memory.*) "... But I'm in darkness and bereaved of light." (*HE reaches over to her hands and gently shuts the book.*) We can read more later. (*HE takes the book and puts it down. A pause.*) Would you sing for me?

CHRISTINE. If you wish.

THE PHANTOM. Oh I do. Very much.

(*SHE looks away.*)

THE PHANTOM. I'm sorry, is there something wrong?

CHRISTINE. (*SHE turns back. Stares at him.*) If I sing for you, will you grant me a favor?

THE PHANTOM. No.

CHRISTINE. (*Startled.*) ... Why?

THE PHANTOM. Because one must sing for love and joy not gain. I will grant you a favor regardless of what you do. Tell me what you wish.

CHRISTINE. (*Warm, loving.*) Let me see your face.

(*Her request takes HIS breath away. It takes him a moment to collect himself.*)

THE PHANTOM. You have asked, I'm afraid, the only thing in my power that I cannot grant. Please, don't ask it again.

CHRISTINE. I've seen your eyes, and I know your heart. Why not let me know your face as well?

THE PHANTOM. Because ... I have no face. I have only the semblance of a face. No one should ever have to look at it.

CHRISTINE. I could look at it.

THE PHANTOM. Stop!

CHRISTINE. I could.

THE PHANTOM. I ask you, please, to stop.

CHRISTINE. Only if you say that you don't love me will I stop.

THE PHANTOM. I think perhaps we should go back, I feel a chill descending. Autumn is approaching! I think it's going to rain today! (*HE starts to gather things.*)

CHRISTINE. Maestro, please.

THE PHANTOM. You don't know what you ask!

CHRISTINE. But I do! *Please.* You have given me so much. Let me at least give you this.

THE PHANTOM. Listen to me, Christina Daeé. This gentle morning stroll with you is the closest I have ever been to bliss. I am satisfied with this.

CHRISTINE. But there's *more*!

THE PHANTOM. I am sure. But not for me.

CHRISTINE. I ask nothing that has not already been done!

[Music Cue #18: MY TRUE LOVE]

(*HE stares at her, stunned. HE backs away a step, scared.*)

CHRISTINE. (*Loving but strong.*) Your mother saw your face and smiled. If love could let her gaze at you and smile ... why can't it do the same for me?

(*HE stares at her, wanting to believe.*
... But he can't. HE puts his hands to his temples and squeezes, as if his head were suddenly bursting open, and this could stop it.
MUSIC.)

CHRISTINE.
MY TRUE LOVE—LOST IN A SHADOWPLAY
I WILL FIND A WAY
THROUGH FEAR AND DOUBT

I WILL FIND YOU OUT IN THE SECRET PLACES
  YOU HIDE ABOUT.

NO, MY LOVE—MORE THAN A FANTASY
YOU MUST BE FOR ME
I'LL HEAR YOUR VOICE, AND I'LL SEE YOUR
  BROW
AND I'LL KNOW YOUR FACE LIKE YOUR
  MUSIC...

CAN YOU HEAR ME NOW? CAN WE MAKE A
  VOW?
EVER TO BE FAITHFUL
I WILL SHOW YOU HOW.

MY TRUE LOVE—OPEN AND TURN TO ME
WHAT NO ONE CAN SEE
YOUR DEEPEST DREAMS OF YOUR DARKEST
  NIGHTS
AND YOUR EYES LIKE LIGHTS
EVER BURNING.

*(HE stops walking and stares back at her. Is it possible?
   What she asks?)*

I WILL HEAR YOUR VOICE
AND I'LL SEE YOUR BROW
LET ME KNOW YOUR FACE
LET ME KNOW IT NOW ... NOW!

(SHE walks toward him. HE does not back away.)

MY TRUE LOVE—LOST IN A SHADOWPLAY
I WILL FIND A WAY
THROUGH FEAR AND DOUBT
I WILL FIND YOU OUT
LET ME KNOW YOUR FACE

LET ME KNOW IT
NOW.
NOW.
NOW!

[Music Cue #18A: UNMASKING]

(Facing her, with his back to us, HE removes his mask.
SHE stares.
SHE backs away, stunned.
And then SHE starts to scream in horror.
HE drops the mask, shattered.
SHE flees. In doing so, SHE runs into the opera flats.
   The TREES come tumbling down. Everything comes
   tumbling down.
As it does, his ACOLYTES flee fearfully into the
   shadows.
HE reaches down with an icy calm, picks up his mask,
   and puts it on.
CHRISTINE races up the stairs and disappears.
HE looks around at his crumbled world.
And then HE SCREAMS to the heavens—a scream that
   echoes through all the corridors and levels of his
   cavernous domain.
And then, with a murderous cry, HE attacks what
   remains of this sham kingdom and tears it down.
Horrid, glaring LIGHT breaks through, glaring down at
   him through grates high above, putting shadows on the
   floor like the bars of a cell. No more flattering shapes
   or colors left, drapes all gone, his domain is revealed
   for what it really is—an ugly, rat infested sewer, skulls
   and bones and rocks and mud.)

[Music Cue #19: MY MOTHER BORE ME]

THE PHANTOM. *(HE sings.)*
MY MOTHER BORE ME IN THE SOUTHERN WILD

I LIVE IN DARKNESS BUT MY SOUL IS LIGHT
LIGHT AS THE FOREHEAD OF AN ENGLISH
   CHILD
BUT I'M IN DARKNESS AND BEREAVED OF
   LIGHT.

MY MOTHER TAUGHT ME UNDERNEATH A TREE
AND SITTING DOWN BEFORE THE HEAT OF DAY
SHE TOOK ME ON HER LAP AND KISSED ME
AND, POINTING TO THE EAST, BEGAN TO SAY:

LOOK UPON THE RISING SUN, THERE GOD DOES
   LIVE
AND GIVES HIS LIGHT AND GIVES HIS HEAT
   AWAY.
AND ALL THE TREES AND FLOWERS AND
   BEASTS AND MEN RECEIVE
THEIR COMFORT FROM THE MORNING
   THROUGH THE BRIGHT NOONDAY.

AND WE ARE PUT ON EARTH A LITTLE SPACE
THAT WE MAY LEARN TO BEAR THE BEAMS OF
   LOVE
AND THESE POOR BODIES, AND THIS WRETCHED
   FACE
ARE BUT A CLOUD, AND LIKE A SHADY GROVE.

FOR WHEN OUR SOULS HAVE LEARNED THE
   HEAT TO BEAR
THE CLOUDS WILL VANISH, WE WILL HEAR HIS
   VOICE
SAYING, COME OUT FROM THE GROVE MY LOVE
   AND CARE
AND ROUND MY GOLDEN TENT LIKE LAMBS
   REJOICE.
THUS DID MY MOTHER SAY, AND KISSED ME
AND THUS I SAY TO LITTLE ENGLISH BOY

WHEN WE ARE BOTH FROM LIGHT AND DARK
   CLOUDS FREE
AND ROUND THE TENT OF GOD WE BOTH
   REJOICE

I WILL SHADE HIM FROM THE HEAT TILL HE
   CAN BEAR
TO LEAN IN JOY UPON OUR FATHER'S KNEE
AND THEN I'LL STAND AND STROKE HIS SILVER
   HAIR
AND BE LIKE HIM, AND HE WILL THEN LOVE
   ME...

VOICES IN MY NIGHTS WILL CRY CHRISTINE
AND EVERY DROP OF RAIN THAT FALLS
WILL BE CHRISTINE.
YOU WERE THE ONLY ONE
MY ONLY CHANCE AT HAPPINESS
MY GOLDEN LEAF OF AUTUMN, MY CHRISTINE.

LOOK WITHIN THIS HEART AND SEE CHRISTINE
THE VERY CONSTANT SOUL AND MUSIC OF
   CHRISTINE
BEHIND THIS MORTAL MASK
THIS TERROR OF A FACE CONCEALS
THE GESTURE AND THE GRACE OF YOU,
   CHRISTINE.

NO ONE ELSE MUST EVER HAVE CHRISTINE
IF NOT FOR ME, YOU'LL BE FOR NO ONE ELSE,
   CHRISTINE
IF I AM GUILTY I'LL BE GUILTY OF
THAT INNOCENCE WHOSE NAME IS LOVE
AND NEVER, NO YOU'LL NEVER BE
FOR ANYONE EXCEPT FOR ME
I DAMN YOU WHEN I LOVE YOU
AND I LOVE YOU

AND I DAMN YOU
MY—
CHRISTINE!

(HE runs off. LIGHTS to BLACK.
[Music Cue #19A: POST ARIA]
LIGHTS UP on Christine's dressing room. The COUNT
de Chandon sits slumped in a chair, in despair.
JEAN-CLAUDE looks in on him.)

JEAN-CLAUDE. ... Monsieur, please, they're
doing everything they can.
THE COUNT. (*Staring out—numb.*) He brought
her in here ... I know it.

(JEAN-CLAUDE shakes his head with sympathy and
leaves the dressing room. HE passes CHOLET in the
hallway.)

CHOLET. Have you seen Carlotta?
JEAN-CLAUDE. (*As HE exits.*) No.
CHOLET. (*Looks in on the Count. To the Count.*)
Have you seen Carlotta?

(The COUNT shakes his head no.)

CHOLET. (*Exits, calling as he does ...*) Carlotta ...!
Carlotta ...!

(The COUNT, alone again, buries his head in his hands.
Suddenly, a WOMAN'S dim shape can be seen through
the full-length mirror. The COUNT does not notice it.
This PERSON moves against the rear of the glass. It's
CHRISTINE! SHE looks ghostly, through the glass.)

CHRISTINE. (*Barely audible.*) Philippe ...

(HE looks up. Is he dreaming?)

CHRISTINE. (*Desperate.*) ... Philippe!

(HE turns to the mirror, sees the ghostly image of Christine and jumps up in terror. SHE starts banging on the rear of the mirror.)

THE COUNT. ... *Christine*? (*HE stares at the glass. How can this be?*)
CHRISTINE. Philippe, help me!
THE COUNT. Oh my God! Christine ... ! (*HE runs to the mirror and tries to figure out how to open it.*)
CHRISTINE. (*Overlapping his action and dialogue.*) Hurry, Philippe! Hurry! (*Etc.*)

(HE runs out to the hallway. Note that most of the following dialogue overlaps.)

[Music Cue #19B: CHASE II]

THE COUNT. Help! Jean-Claude! Ledoux! Someone! Hurry! It's Christine! HELP! IT'S CHRISTINE! *(The COUNT runs back in and continues to try to open the mirror.)* It must be a panel! How do I open it?
CHRISTINE. I think there's a button.
THE COUNT. Where, where?
CHRISTINE. I don't know! On the side I think. Hurry, hurry!

(JEAN-CLAUDE and CARRIERE rush in.)

CARRIERE. (*Sees what's happening.*) Step aside!

(HE runs to the mirror, presses the proper spot. The mirror opens. CHRISTINE is standing there, pale as a ghost.)

CHRISTINE. Oh Philippe! *(SHE runs into the Count's arms.)*

THE COUNT. Christine, Christine!

CARRIERE. What happened?

CHRISTINE. *I saw his face.*

CARRIERE. Oh God!

CHRISTINE. I *asked* him to let me see it. And he did.

CARRIERE. *(To the Count.)* Get her out of here. *Hurry*!

CHRISTINE. *(To the Count, as HE guides her out.)* ... No! ... No! ... *(To the Count, in the hallway.)* I thought I could look at his face. He *believed* in me... ! *(A sudden revelation.)* I should go back down. I should make amends!

CARRIERE. It's too late for that! Get her out of here!

(THEY exit down the hall.
CARRIERE runs to a POLICEMAN.)

CARRIERE. Get everyone out of the building!

POLICEMAN. *(As if Carriere were mad.)* What are you talking about?

CARRIERE. Just do it! HURRY!

(CARRIERE runs off. The POLICEMAN stares after him, puzzled.
During this encounter, the PHANTOM has emerged through the panel in Christine's dressing room. His mask is a death's head again, but bejeweled, like a jade Aztec skull, the mask of an avenging god, both beauteous and terrifying at the same time.

*The PHANTOM emerges from Christine's dressing room
    and approaches the policeman from behind. As he
    does, Christine's dressing room flies away.*

*The POLICEMAN turns. Gasps. Goes for his gun. The
    PHANTOM strikes the policeman's gun hand with his
    sword cane, then strikes him a blow to the neck.*

*The POLICEMAN collapses. The PHANTOM starts to
    drag him into a room when FLORA, FLORENCE and
    FLEURE emerge from another room, see him and start
    screaming for help.*

POLICE run on.

*The PHANTOM grabs one of the POLICE as a shield and
    starts to escape. Some of the POLICE shoot. The
    MAN held as a shield is hit. The PHANTOM lets him
    go and runs off. As he does, another shot rings out.
    HE's hit in the side.*

*CARRIERE runs on in time to see ERIK flee, badly
    wounded.*

LEDOUX runs on.)

LEDOUX. What! What?
A POLICEMAN. He was here!
LEDOUX. You had him and you let him get away!?
A POLICEMAN. But I hit him!
LEDOUX. Well, at least we know he's up here. (*To
the other police.*) All right, spread out!

*(THEY do. SOME rush off. SOME stay to attend to the
    fallen policeman.)*

A POLICEMAN. Look! Some blood!

*(Suddenly, a SCREAM is heard. ALL turn towards the
    sound. Enter, CHOLET, wailing with grief.)*

CHOLET. Carlotta... ! My wife... ! I found her ...!

(LIGHTS to BLACK.
In the dark we hear TWO GUNSHOTS.
LIGHTS UP. The stage has changed. We are in the
*   BACKSTAGE area. Pieces of scenery from an opera*
*   are scattered about. Lots of SHADOWS and eerie,*
*   shadowy places. LEDOUX and the POLICE, guns out*
*   and ready, are searching everywhere, scared.*
*   CARRIERE is with them, scared in a different way.)*

LEDOUX. *(Staring at the floor.)* More blood. He
can't be far.

(Another GUNSHOT offstage. LEDOUX and his MEN
*   go off in pursuit.)*

THE PHANTOM'S VOICE. *(Weak—barely*
audible.) ... Gerard ... ? *(CARRIERE looks all around,*
startled.) Over here. In back. Hurry.

(CARRIERE turns toward some opera flats and a dark
*   area beyond. As he does, LEDOUX and the POLICE*
*   head back towards Carriere.)*

LEDOUX. *(To his men.)* He's got to be nearby.
There's blood everywhere. Search behind that scenery.
CARRIERE. *(To Ledoux.)* I just did! He's not here.
LEDOUX. *(To his men.)* All right. We'll try up here.

(THEY exit. CARRIERE immediately moves to the flats
*   and pulls them aside enough to step through. The*
*   PHANTOM is lying against some props, his shirt*
*   bloody. HE's been badly hit.)*

CARRIERE. Erik!
THE PHANTOM. It's all right.

(CARRIERE lifts his son's head and cradles it. The PHANTOM winces.)

THE PHANTOM. ... Can you get me back down?
CARRIERE. Yes. But not yet.

(POLICE enter. The PHANTOM and CARRIERE wait till they're gone. Once THEY are ....)

CARRIERE. ... Is there a way down from here?

[Music Cue #19C: FATHER/SON RECONCILIATION]

THE PHANTOM. *(Having difficulty breathing.)* No, but nearby. We'll have to cross the stage.

*(CARRIERE scans the area. It's too dangerous to move right now. POLICE are in the vicinity.
The PHANTOM coughs up some blood. CARRIERE turns and stares back at his son. There's nothing to do but wait.)*

THE PHANTOM. *(Finally; enough strength again to talk.)* ... By the way, I'm sorry about before. *(CARRIERE looks at him, mystified.)* Getting ... angry at you.
CARRIERE. *(Warm smile.)* ... I understood.

(The PHANTOM moves slightly and winces. With difficulty, HE shifts position to something more comfortable.)

THE PHANTOM. All in all ... it wasn't so bad ... Being born, I mean. *(Pause.)* Because I could hear music.
CARRIERE. ... Yes.
THE PHANTOM. *And I heard Christine!*

CARRIERE. She didn't mean to hurt you.

THE PHANTOM. I know that. I'm sorry that I frightened her. She asked a bit too much of me, that's all. Not her fault. She thought she loved me.

CARRIERE. She *does*.

THE PHANTOM. She *did* ... But only for a moment. Well! That's not bad—a moment such as that. Worth living for, I think.

CARRIERE. She was unprepared for you.

THE PHANTOM. (*Shaking his head no.*) She was unprepared for ugliness. (*Pause.*) And for a brief sweet moment, so was I. (*Pause.*) Well, I'm glad she saw. Fitting end to my illusions. (*HE takes off his death's head mask. Another mask is underneath. His "normal" mask.*) ... Perhaps *you'd* like to see.

CARRIERE. See what?

THE PHANTOM. My face.

CARRIERE. I've already seen your face.

THE PHANTOM. ... When?

CARRIERE. When you were a child.

THE PHANTOM. A toddler!

CARRIERE. Yes.

THE PHANTOM. Did you know my mother *well*?

CARRIERE. ... Yes.

THE PHANTOM. Did you love her?

CARRIERE. Oh yes.

THE PHANTOM. (*Astonished.*) And she let you see my face?

CARRIERE. She thought your face was absolutely and flawlessly *beautiful*.

THE PHANTOM. Ahhhh!

CARRIERE. I'm sorry.

THE PHANTOM. (*Recovering.*) No ... No, that's all right. I knew she did. I ... can remember her expression ... I *think*.

(*The PHANTOM stares off, remembering.*

[Music Cue #20: YOU ARE MY OWN]

CARRIERE. (*Sings.*)
ERIK YOU ARE MY SON
DO YOU KNOW YOU'RE MY SON?
YOU BECAME MY WHOLE LIFE
WHEN YOUR LIFE WAS BEGUN
DO YOU KNOW THAT THE MAN
WHO PROTECTED YOU ALWAYS
HAS BEEN YOUR FATHER?
THE PHANTOM.
YES, I KNOW I'M YOUR SON
AND I MORE THAN SURMISE
I HAVE KNOWN FOR SOME YEARS
THAT MY EYES ARE YOUR EYES
AND I'VE WONDERED HOW LONG IT WOULD
   TAKE YOU
TO TELL ME IT'S TRUE.
CARRIERE.
NOW THAT YOU KNOW, I MUST TELL YOU I'M
   GRATEFUL FOR YOU.
THE PHANTOM.
NO, IT IS I WHO AM GRATEFUL
TO YOU, MY FATHER.
BOTH.
FOR THE MUSIC ALONE
IT'S BEEN WORTH ALL THE PAIN
AND A LIFE OF PERPETUAL DARKNESS AND
   RAIN
CARRIERE.
FOR INSIDE YOU THE LIGHT OF THE SOUL OF
   YOUR MOTHER HAS SHONE
ERIK YOU ARE MY SON, AND MY BOY, AND MY
   LIFE, AND MY OWN.

(The MUSIC continues under.)

THE PHANTOM. ... And what did *you* think of it?
CARRIERE. Think of what?
THE PHANTOM. Your infant's face.

(A pause.)

   CARRIERE. (*Finally.*) ... It could have been better.

(The PHANTOM laughs.)

   THE PHANTOM. ... Remember the day I looked
down in the water?
   CARRIERE. Yes.
   THE PHANTOM. (*With a laugh.*) I thought I'd
seen a sea monster!
   CARRIERE. I remember.
   THE PHANTOM. I had, that's the irony. Then, for
a while, I thought I was just dreaming.
   CARRIERE. I went through that phase, too.
   THE PHANTOM. Not a good face for a tenor, I
remember thinking!
   CARRIERE. Not even for a baritone.
   THE PHANTOM. It *is* a good voice, isn't it?
   CARRIERE. (*Warm smile.*) Very good. You'd have
had a fine career.
   THE PHANTOM. (*Sings.*)
WILL YOU BURY ME DEEP
I MUST NEVER BE FOUND.
WHEN AT LAST I FIND SLEEP
AND I'M COLD IN THE GROUND.
   CARRIERE.
YES, I PROMISE I'LL NEVER ALLOW YOU
TO BE ON DISPLAY.
ERIK, YOU ARE MY SON.
   THE PHANTOM.
I HAVE KNOWN ALL ALONG.

CARRIERE.
AND THE LIGHT OF MY LIFE—
  THE PHANTOM.
I HAVE KNOWN ALL ALONG.
  CARRIERE.
ERIK, YOU ARE MY SON, AND MY BOY,
AND MY LOVE, AND MY OWN!

(MUSIC ends.)

  CARRIERE. Come, I'll help you back down.
  THE COUNT. (*From the shadows*.) Here he is!

(The COUNT enters with CHRISTINE.)

[Music Cue #21: CHASE III]

  CHRISTINE. Erik!
  THE PHANTOM. (*Turning towards the sound.*)
Christine?
  THE COUNT. (*Calling towards off-stage.*)
HURRY!
  THE PHANTOM. (*Advancing on the Count.*) Let
her go.
  CARRIERE. (*Tries to stop him.*) Erik ...
  THE PHANTOM. (*Breaks free of Carriere's grasp.*)
She saw my face. *She is mine*!
  CARRIERE. Erik!
  THE COUNT. (*To Christine.*) Run.
  CHRISTINE. No!

(The PHANTOM draws his sword cane.)

  THE COUNT. I said RUN!
  CARRIERE. (*In terror.*) Erik!
  CHRISTINE. (*To the Phantom, re Philippe.*)
Please! He means you no harm.

THE PHANTOM. I said let her go!

*(The PHANTOM takes a swipe at the COUNT, who
leaps aside just in time.*
*The pain causes the PHANTOM to flinch and lose focus
for a moment. The COUNT springs at him and knocks
the sword from his hand. THEY struggle.)*

VOICES. *(From off-stage.)* There he is! / He's over
here! / This way! This way!

*(POLICE run on. As they do, the PHANTOM breaks
free, runs to some stairs and starts to ascend.*
*The COUNT runs up after him. THEY start to fight on
the stairs. As they struggle, LEDOUX and the
POLICE race on, guns out.)*

LEDOUX. Don't shoot. Take him! ... DON'T
SHOOT! You could hit Monsieur le Count.

(Some POLICE start to ascend the stairs.
Down below, CARRIERE looks on in terror.
*The PHANTOM breaks free of the Count's grasp and
races, as best he can, up to the catwalk. The COUNT
pursues him.)*

CHRISTINE. *(To Carriere, during the above.)* I said
I could look at his face ... He trusted me! I let him down!
I betrayed his trust! This is all my fault!

(Meanwhile, POLICE ascend from another side.)

LEDOUX. *(Shouting upwards.)* Monsieur le Count!
Let the police handle this!

(The COUNT stops.

*The PHANTOM spots a POLICEMAN approaching with
a gun out. The PHANTOM runs over to the policeman
and, in a fight, gets the man's gun away. Holding the
gun on the policeman, the PHANTOM backs away
and...
...into the Count. The PHANTOM and the COUNT
fight. The fight takes them closer and closer to the
edge.
Suddenly, PHILIPPE slips and tumbles. HE looks like
he's about to fall.)*

CHRISTINE. No!

*(But the COUNT catches himself just as he's about to fall
off.)*

CHRISTINE. *Philippe ...!*

*(PHILIPPE is dangling by his hands from the catwalk.
The PHANTOM bends. HE starts to break the Count's
grip.
One of the POLICE starts to shoot.)*

LEDOUX. Stop, you fool! You could hit Monsieur le
Count!
CHRISTINE. Philippe! On no!

(ERIK looks down at CHRISTINE, staring up.)

CHRISTINE. *(To the Phantom.)* Please ...

*(ERIK hesitates. HE looks down. PHILIPPE is starting
to lose his grip; only one hand holding now. ERIK
reaches down, takes the Count's hand and helps him
up.)*

CHRISTINE. *(With relief.)* Philippe ...!

(ERIK looks down at Christine. Then HE turns and stares at the Count. The COUNT stares back at Erik, not sure what to do.
For a moment, nothing else happens—it's just these TWO MEN, staring at each other.
Then the COUNT backs away a step. HE will not try to capture the Phantom, or harm him.
The POLICEMAN near Ledoux takes aim and shoots.
Another POLICEMAN also shoots. Both shots ricochet off the catwalk.)

LEDOUX. I SAID NOT TO SHOOT!
POLICEMAN. But I had a clear shot!
LEDOUX. It could ricochet and hit one of our men! We can get closer! (*To his other men.*) Go up both sides.
CHRISTINE. (*Climbing up spiral stairs.*) Let me speak with him! Please, don't shoot him! Erik! Listen to me!

(POLICE rush past her; SHE turns and goes back down.)

POLICEMEN. What's he up to?/ What's he doing?

(ALL look up. ERIK is standing at the railing. It looks like HE's about to leap to his death, but HE's got hold of a rope.)

CHRISTINE. (*Looking up.*) My God! No!

(HE swings from the catwalk toward a railing across the stage.
ERIK almost grabs the railing he needs. But HE misses. HE begins to swing back and forth, high above, helplessly.)

LEDOUX. (*To his men.*) He's got no way out. We can get him alive!

(*CARRIERE hears that with horror.*)

POLICE. (*Calling across the space.*) We're going to get him alive!/ Lower him in!/ Where's the rigging? / Over there!

(*THEY close in on him. SOME prepare to grab his rope with poles and other ropes. ERIK looks down like a trapped animal. HE stares at the police in terror. Then HE turns to his father.*)

THE PHANTOM. Gerard, HELP ME! Please, you promised!

(*CARRIERE looks up, unsure of what he could possibly do. The rope the Phantom is holding onto is swinging less. HE is about to be caught.*)

THE PHANTOM. (*Reaching out towards his father.*) ... Please!

(*CARRIERE runs to a policeman and grabs his gun. The POLICEMAN struggles but CARRIERE aims the gun at him.*)

CARRIERE. Get back!
POLICE. LOOK OUT!/ HE'S GOT A GUN!

(*CARRIERE looks up at Erik.*)

THE PHANTOM. ... Yes.

(*CARRIERE, in horror, aims the gun at Erik.*)

LEDOUX. Gerard! My God! What are you doing!?
THE PHANTOM. (*To his father.*) Yes! (*But CARRIERE can't bring himself to do it.*) ... Do it! *Please!*

(LEDOUX starts running toward Carriere.)

LEDOUX. (*To Carriere, as he runs.*) No, no, Gerard, are you mad! We can get him alive!
THE PHANTOM. (*To his father.*) HURRY!

(Just before Ledoux reaches Carriere, or the other police reach the Phantom with their poles and ropes, CARRIERE shoots. ERIK is hit.)

THE PHANTOM. *Christiiiiiiine!*

[Music Cue #22: FINALE ACT II]

(HE falls along the rope to the ground below. SCREAMS from everywhere, but especially from CHRISTINE, who rushes towards him.)

CHRISTINE. No! No! Erik!
CARRIERE. (*To Ledoux.*) Ledoux, my friend, please get your men back. Leave me with him. I'll explain later. (*LEDOUX hesitates.*) Please. *Please.* PLEASE!
LEDOUX. Gerard, I can't!

(CARRIERE whispers something to Ledoux. It's enough for LEDOUX to understand. HE stares at Carriere in both horror and compassion.)

LEDOUX. (*Turning to his men.*) Get back. Get back. (*THEY exit.*)
THE PHANTOM. (*Barely audible.*) *Christine ...*

(*The PHANTOM reaches up to her face and touches it
   softly.
SHE reaches down and touches his mask.
HE tries to pull away.*)

THE PHANTOM. No! Please ... *Please*!

(*SHE starts to remove his mask.*)

THE PHANTOM. No ... !

(*HE tries to put the mask back on but he can't. SHE
   gazes down. [Note: we still must not see his face; at
   most, we can see a small part of it.]*)

THE PHANTOM. Christine ...

(*MUSIC. Reprise of THE MUSIC LESSON.*)

CHRISTINE.
OH, YOU ARE MUSIC
BEAUTIFUL MUSIC
AND YOU ARE LIGHT TO ME.

OH YOU ARE MUSIC
MOONBEAMS OF MUSIC
AND YOU ARE LIFE TO ME.
      THE PHANTOM. Ahhhhhh! Christine.

(*CHRISTINE bends and kisses him on the forehead. HIS
   hand relaxes. With a great, gentle sigh, HE dies.*)

SHE stares down at him. And then, slowly, SHE puts his
    mask back on.
PHILIPPE comes up and takes CHRISTINE away.
CARRIERE returns, bends down and cradles his son's
    body.)

SLOW CURTAIN

[Music Cue #23: BOWS]

[Music Cue #24: EXIT]

COSTUME PLOT

ACT I

SCENE A: AVENUE L'OPERA – "Melodie de Paris"

Christine: striped blouse, brown skirt, cummerbund

Count: purple cutaway, lavender gloves, brocade vest, grey pants, tux shirt

Lead Tenor: beige day suit, vest, cream ascot, shirt, straw boater

Fem. #1: beige day suit, straw hat, purse

Fem. #2: blue day suit with velvet collar, dickie, straw hat, gloves

Fem. #3: (girlfriend) peach/blue dress, cape, straw hat, gloves, bag

Fem. #4: (girlfriend) gray/green satin dress, hat, gloves, bag

Fem. #5: silver/blue satin dress w/ruffled sleeves, hat, gloves, bag

Fem. #6: blue skirt, pink striped blouse, straw hat, gloves, bag

Fem. #7: linen-color day suit, dickie, hat, gloves, purse

Fem. #8: gray/black dress, hat, gloves, bag

Male #1: bicyclist: cream day suit, rust vest, tie, straw boater, shirt

Male #2: musician: plaid pants, rust vest, white shirt, beret

Male #3: artist: plaid pants, beige shirt, blue smock, bowtie, navy beret

Male #4: puppeteer: gray pants, striped vest, cream shirt, purple tie, cap

Male #5: juggler: navy pants, red vest, white shirt, gray cap

Male #6: bread vendor: gray pants, orange/white striped shirt, apron, sleeve garters

Male #7: wealthy man: 3-piece brown day suit, ascot, brown top hat, cream shirt, gloves

Male #8: wealthy man: 3-piece gray day suit, striped tie, straw boater, cream shirt, gloves

Male #9: wealthy man: 3-piece day suit, bowtie, cream shirt, gloves

Male #10: wealthy man: 3-piece frock suit, gray top hat, brocade vest, ascot, white shirt, gloves

Male #11: blue/gray frock coat, gray pants, white shirt, satin vest, red ascot, gray gloves

Male #12: navy frock coat, black pants, red vest, white shirt, gray ascot

SCENE B: STAIRWELL IN THE CATACOMBS

Buquet: brown pinstripe pants, brown brocade vest, gray cutaway coat, tie

SCENE C: PHANTOM'S ROOM – "Paris is a Tomb"

Phantom: black period tail suit, black and white satin cape, mask, shirt

Acolyte: rag clothing

Acolyte: rag clothing

Buquet: as before

SCENE D: HALL OF MIRRORS – "Dressing for the Night"

Carlotta: red/black lace dress, red feather headpiece, black boa, fan, long black velvet gloves

Carriere: gray frock coat, gray vest, black tux pants, black top hat, gray ascot, tux shirt

Jean-Claude: brown pinstripe pants, brown brocade vest, gray cutaway coat, tie

Cholet: black frock coat, black vest, black and white satin cravat, tux pants, tux shirt

Fem. #1: black v-neck dress w/satin trim, black gloves, feather headpiece, black cape

Fem. #2: black dress w/sequins, black gloves, feather headpiece, black cape

Fem. #3: purple/black dress, black gloves, headpiece, cape

Fem. #4: purple iridescent dress w/ white lace, black gloves, headpiece, black cape

Fem. #5: light purple dress w/black appliques, black gloves, headpiece, black cape

Fem. #6: black/rose dress, black gloves, headpiece, black cape

Fem. #7: black metallic lace dress, black gloves, headpiece, cape

Fem. #8: Diva: gray metallic robe, "titania" wig, headpiece

Male #7: black tail suit, white vest, tux shirt, white gloves, bowtie

Male #8: black tail suit, white vest, tux shirt, white gloves, bowtie

Male #9: black tail suit, white vest, tux shirt, white gloves, bowtie

Male #10: black tail suit, white vest, tux shirt, white gloves, bowtie

Male #11: black tail suit, white vest, tux shirt, white gloves, bowtie

Male #12: black tail suit, white vest, tux shirt, white gloves, bowtie

SCENE E: MANAGER'S OFFICE
Carriere: as before
Cholet: as before

SCENE F: NETWORK OF CORRIDORS – "Where is the Path"/ "Where in the World"
Phantom: as before
Carriere: as before
Acolytes 1-4: in rags

SCENE J: OFF STAGE IN THE WINGS

Christine: brown striped overblouse, skirt as before, straw hat
Jean-Claude: as before
Fem. #1: Florence: lace peignoir, blue corset, bloomers
Fem. #2 Fleure: lace peignoir, pink corset, bloomers
Fem. #7: Flora: mauve velvet robe, peach corset, bloomers

SCENE K: MANAGER'S OFFICE – "Mine"
Carlotta: green velvet dress and petticoat
Cholet: as before
Music Dir: as before (Sc. A)
Costumer: frock coat, pants, cravat

SCENE L1 & L2: ONSTAGE – "Home" (Christine)
Christine: Victorian ivory blouse, same skirt, ribbon cummerbund
Fem. #3: bloomers, corset, lace peignoir, lose costume piece

SCENE L3: STAIRWELL IN CATACOMBS – "Home" (Phantom)
Phantom: as before

SCENE L4: ONSTAGE – "Home" (Both)
same

SCENE P: ONSTAGE
Cholet: as before
Ledoux: navy blue and red inspector's uniform, cap, cape

SCENE O 1-3: MUSIC ROOM – "Vocalizing"
Christine: as before, add ivory shawl
Phantom: as before, w/o coat

SCENE R 1-3: MANAGER'S OFFICE
Carlotta: one "opera" costume for each scene, R1-R3

Cholet: same
Ledoux: same
Policeman: police uniform, police hat, gloves
Policeman: police uniform, police hat, gloves

SCENE S: THE OPERA HOUSE – "Phantom Fugue"
Fugue can use almost any variation of policeman, stagehands, performers, depending on the size of your chorus. It should include the Phantom, Phantom double, Carlotta, Ledoux, Cholet.

SCENE T: MUSIC ROOM – "You are Music"
Christine: blue print and eyelet two-piece dress
Phantom: as before

SCENE U: THE BISTRO – "Sing Can You Sing"
"Paris"/ "Melodie de Paris"
Christine: ivory satin dress, long ivory gloves
Phantom: as before with black/silver cape, hat
Carlotta: yellow with peach roses dress, peach boa
Carriere: black tailcoat, black opera cape, white vest, bowtie, gloves
Jean-Claude: black tailsuit, white vest, white bowtie, black cape
Lead Tenor: black tailsuit, white vest, white bowtie, black cape
Count: black tailsuit, white vest, white bowtie, black cape, honor sash
Buquet: as headwaiter: red vest, black tailsuit, tux shirt, bowtie, white gloves
Cholet: black tailsuit, white vest, white satin cravat, black double cape, black top hat, white gloves
Fem. #1: Florence: light blue sequin dress, blue gloves, blue feather boa, headpiece
Fem. #2: Fleure: rose/gray lace dress, black gloves, headpiece

Fem. #3: blue lace dress, blue boa, white gloves, headpiece

Fem. #4: lavender satin off-shoulder dress, lavender gloves, headpiece

Fem. #5: gray satin dress, white gloves, fan, headpiece

Fem. #6: lavender/gray satin dress w/cream lace, white gloves, headpiece

Fem. #7: Flora: pink metallic dress w/ white feather sleeves, white gloves, feather headpiece

Fem. #8: large pastel dress, white gloves, headpiece

Male #1-6: waiters: white shirts, aprons, black pants, black/white stripe vest, arm garter, rust bowtie

Male #7-12: same as Scene D

SCENE V: AVENUE L'OPERA – "Who Could Ever Have Dreamed"

Christine: add iridescent blue satin and tulle cape

Count: as before

Male #4: rough pants, cap, shirt, vest

Male #5: rough pants, shirt, cap, vest

Voice parts: same as Scene U.

SCENE W1 – W3: CHRISTINE'S & CARLOTTA'S DRESSING ROOM

Christine: lace peignoir

Carlotta: silver and black lace dress w/feather sleeves

Cholet: as before

SCENE X1 – X5: VARIOUS LOCATIONS ON STAGE – "The Fairy Queen"

Christine: Titania dress

Carlotta: as before

Phantom: as before w/o hat

Jean-Claude: as Scene J

Lead Tenor: Oberon: purple velvet tunic, helmet w/ feathers, cape, tights, sandals

Ledoux: black tailsuit, white vest, bowtie, black cape, tux shirt, white gloves
Cholet: as before
Fem. #1-5: Fairies: white poly dresses, jewelry, headpieces
Fem. #7 Fairy: white poly dresses, jewelry, headpieces
Male #1: Puck: tights, tunic, wreath headpiece
Assorted stagehands and police dressed as in earlier scenes depending on size of chorus.

SCENE Y: CHRISTINE'S DRESSING ROOM
Phantom: as before
Christine: as before
Count: as before

SCENE Z: CATACOMBS/LAGOON – "Where in the World" (Reprise)
Phantom: as before
Christine: as before
Phantom dbl: as Phantom
Christine dbl: as Christine
Acolyte: in robes
Acolyte: in robes

ACT TWO

SCENE AA: LAGOON BENEATH THE OPERA HOUSE – "Without Your Music"
Christine: as before
Phantom: as before
Acolyte: as before

SCENE BB: PHANTOM'S BED CHAMBER – "Without Your Music"
Christine: as before
Phantom: as before

PHANTOM 127

SCENE CC: OUTSIDE THE BED CHAMBER – "Where in the World" (Reprise)
Phantom: as before
Carriere: as before

SCENE DD 1–3: BEDROOM – "Story of Erik"
Christine: as before
Carriere: as before
Fem. #1,2,7: white tutu, colored sashes and chokers, pink tights, trunks
Fem. #3: black/blue dress w/lace
Fem. #4: brown dress w/black trim, black hat, gloves
Fem. #5: gray satin w/red velvet trim
Fem. #6: dark brown dress, hat
Fem. #8: Gypsy: brocade skirt, 3 colorful shawls, white blouse, scarf
Male #7: Young Carriere: 2-piece suit, light vest, cravat, cream suit
Male #8-12: dark frock suit, top hat, cravat, gloves
Male #1-6: Monk robes
Child: cream shirt, knickers, mask

SCENE EE 1–2: CATWALK/STAIRCASE
Carriere: as before
Count: as before
Ledoux: as before
Phantom: black double cape w/red lining, black/red satin hood
Carlotta: red kimono (flameproofed)

SCENE FF: BED CHAMBER
Phantom: black/white satin cape, white "Romeo" shirt
Christine: as before

SCENE GG 1-2: PHANTOM'S PARK – "My True Love" / "My Mother Bore Me"
Phantom: same

Christine: same
Acolytes: as before

SCENE HH 1–4: VARIOUS STAGE LOCATIONS – "Duet" / "You are Music" (Reprise)
Phantom: same
Christine: same
Carriere: same
Jean Claude: same
Count: same
policeman, stagehands, other chorus dressed as needed

PROPERTY PLOT

<u>ACT ONE</u>

<u>SCENE A: AVENUE L'OPERA – "Melodie de Paris"</u>
flower cart
3 jugglers' sandbags
vendor's tray w/masks, pinwheels, etc.
coins
sheet music
painting on easel w/palette, stool
suitcase w/folding legs
Punch and Judy puppets
loaf of bread
parasols
wicker wine basket with bottle and 3 glasses
business cards

<u>SCENE B: STAIRWELL IN THE CATACOMBS</u>
lantern

<u>SCENE C: PHANTOM'S ROOM – "Paris is a Tomb"</u>
armoire for masks
display of Phantom's masks
2 torches
dagger
shattered mirror

<u>SCENE D: HALL OF MIRRORS – "Dressing for the
    Night"</u>
3 chairs
2 dressing tables
champagne glasses
walking sticks
note
fans

SCENE E: MANAGER'S OFFICE
liquor cabinet with dressing
manager's office desk with dressing
chair behind desk
pictures to hang on walls
backless couch

SCENE F: NETWORK OF CORRIDORS – "Where is the Path" / "Where in the World"
no props

SCENE J: OFF STAGE IN THE WINGS
business card
note

SCENE K: MANAGER'S OFFICE –"Mine"
furniture and dressing as before
portfolios
swatch of materials
bolt of fabric
score and manuscripts
letter opener
rack of clothing/costumes

SCENE L1 & L2: ONSTAGE – "Home" (Christine)
mirror on stand
rack of costumes
hamper of costumes

SCENE L3: STAIRWELL IN CATACOMBS – "Home" (Phantom)
no props

SCENE L4: ONSTAGE – "Home" (Both)
same as L1 & L2

SCENE P: ONSTAGE

flat from *Aida*

SCENE Q 1–3: MUSIC ROOM – "Vocalizing"
harpsichord
stool
candelabra

SCENE R 1–3: MANAGER'S OFFICE
liquor cabinet from before without dressing
Buquet's body in cabinet
desk from before with dressing
wig on stick
glasses stuck to tray
Aida spear
newspapers

SCENE S: THE OPERA HOUSE – "Phantom Fugue"
nightclubs for police
guns for police

SCENE T: MUSIC ROOM – "You are Music"
same as before

SCENE U: THE BISTRO – "Sing Can You Sing"
   "Paris" "Melodie de Paris"
two banquets with four chairs each
two tables with four chairs each
champagne glasses
champagne bottles
single stem rose
dressing for tables

SCENE V: AVENUE L'OPERA – "Who Could Ever
   Have Dreamed"
two glasses
champagne bottle
two sandwich boards advertising *The Fairy Queen*

opera programs tickets

SCENE W1 – W3: CHRISTINE'S & CARLOTTA'S DRESSING ROOM

CHRISTINE:
table
sofa
chair
mirror on table
make-up on table

CARLOTTA:
dressing table
chair
2 vials of "poison"
large jeweled glass

SCENE X1 – X5: VARIOUS LOCATIONS ON STAGE – "The Fairy Queen"
fairy dust
sword
thrown programs

SCENE Y: CHRISTINE'S DRESSING ROOM
same as before

SCENE Z: CATACOMBS/LAGOON – "Where in the World" (Reprise)
two torches
lifelike dummy of Christine

ACT TWO

SCENE AA: LAGOON BENEATH THE OPERA HOUSE – "Without Your Music"
Phantom's boat
push pole

SCENE BB: PHANTOM'S BED CHAMBER – "Without Your Music"
bed with headboard
candelabra
"Belladova" portrait on stand

torches
pillows on bed
comforter
shawl

SCENE CC: OUTSIDE THE BED CHAMBER – "Where in the World" (Reprise)
none

SCENE DD 1–3: BEDROOM – "Story of Erik"
ballet mirror
manuscripts
blanket
fake "baby"
powders
herbs

SCENE EE 1–2: CATWALK/STAIRCASE
rubber gloves
electric cable
bouquet of flowers

SCENE FF: BED CHAMBER
same as before

SCENE GG 1–2: PHANTOM'S PARK – "My True Love" / "My Mother Bore Me"
picnic basket
wine bottle and two glasses
book of poetry

SCENE HH 1–4: VARIOUS STAGE LOCATIONS – "Duet" / "You are Music" (Reprise)
clothes hamper
dagger
pistol

SCENE DESIGN

"PHANTOM"

(OPENING, ACT I)

AVENUE L'OPERA DROP

BLACK SCRIM

U.S. EDGE RAKED DECK

U.S. GUIDE TRACK

S.L. GUIDE TRACKS

S.R. GUIDE TRACKS

PUPPET THEATRE

CATWALK

MASKING SLIDERS L+R

PAINT STAND

ESCAPE TOWERS STAIR & LANDING L.+ R.

PALETTE TRACK

SUITCASE

BOAT GUIDE TRACK

D.S. EDGE RAKED DECK

Other Publications for Your Interest

MAIL
(ADVANCED GROUPS—MUSICAL)
Book & Lyrics by JERRY COLKER
Music by MICHAEL RUPERS

9 men, 6 women—2 Sets

What a terrific idea for a "concept musical"! As *Mail* opens Alex, an unpublished novelist, is having an acute anxiety attack over his lack of success in writing and his indecision regarding his girlfriend, Dana; so, he "hits the ground running" and doesn't come back for 4 months! When Alex finally returns to his apartment, he finds an unending stream of messages on his answering machine and stacks and stacks of unopened mail. As he opens his mail, it in effect comes to life, as we learn what has been happening with Alex's friends, and with Dana, during his absence. There is also some hilarious junk mail, which bombards Alex muscially, as well as unpaid bills from the likes of the electric company (the ensemble comes dancing out of Alex's refrigerator singing "We're Gonna Turn Off Your Juice"). In the second act, we move into a sort of abstract vision of Alex's world, a blank piece of paper upon which he can, if he is able, and if he wishes, start over—with his writing, with his friends, with his father and, maybe, with Dana. Producers looking for something wild and crazy will, we know, want to open *this* MAIL, a hit with audiences and critics coast-to-coast, from the authors of THREE GUYS NAKED FROM THE WAIST DOWN! "At least 12 songs are solid enough to stand on their own. If MAIL can't deliver, there is little hope for the future of the musical theatre, unless we continue to rely on the British to take possession of a truly American art form."—Drama-Logue. "Make room for the theatre's newest musical geniuses."—The Same. (Terms quoted on application. Music available on rental. See p. 48.)

CHESS
(ADVANCED GROUPS—MUSICAL/OPERA)
Book by RICHARD NELSON
Lyrics by TIM RICE
Music by BJORN ULVAEUS & BENNY ANDERSSON

9 men, 2 women, 1 female child, plus ensemble

A *musical* about an *international chess match*?!?! A bad idea from the get-go, you'd think; but no—Tim Rice (he of *Evita, Joseph and the Amazing Technicolor Dreamcoat* and *Jesus Christ Superstar*), Bjorn Ulvaeus and Benny Andersson (they of Swedish Supergroup ABBA) and noted American playwright Richard Nelson, all in collaboration with Trevor Nunn (*Les Miz., Nick Nick*, etc.) have pulled it off, creating an extraordinary rock opera about international intrigue which uses as a metaphor a media-drenched chess match between a loutish American champion (shades of Bobby Fischer) and a nice-guy Soviet champion. The American has a girlfriend, Florence, there in Bangkok (where the match takes place) to be his second and to provide moral support. There she meets, and falls in love with, Anatoly, the Soviet champion—and the sparks fly, particularly when Anatoly decides to defect to the west, causing a postponement and change of venue to Budapest. Eventually, it is clear that all the characters are merely pawns in a larger chess match between the C.I.A. and the KGB! The pivotal role of Florence is perhaps the most extraordinary and complex role in the musical theatre since Eva Peron; and the roles of Freddie and Anatoly (both tenors) are great, too. Several of the songs have become international hits, including Florence's "Heaven Help My Heart", "I know Him So Well" and "Nobody's On Nobody's Side", and Freddie's descent into the maelstrom of decadence, "One Night in Bangkok". Playing to full houses and standing ovations, *Chess* closed exceedingly prematurely on Broadway; and, perhaps the story behind *that* just might make the basis of another Rice/ABBA/Nelson/Nunn collaboration! (Terms quoted on application. Music available on rental. See p. 48.) Slightly restricted.

(#5236)

Other Publications for Your Interest

THREE GUYS NAKED FROM THE WAIST DOWN
(ADVANCED GROUPS—MUSICAL)
Book & Lyrics by JERRY COLKER
Music by MICHAEL RUPERT

3 men—Unit Set

This is a show about stand-up comics; and doing stand-up is, literally, like being in front of a crowd naked from the waist down. It is a painful transformation of one's innermost secrets into something funny. Does this show sound "serious"? It is. It's wild and crazy, too. We follow the careers of three comics who unite to form an '80's version of the Three Stooges, intellectual and slapstick all at the same time; and very, very hip. Think of "Saturday Night Live", Bill Murray, Eddie Murphy, Andy Kaufman, George Karlin and the "new wave". This is the familiar rags-to-riches-to-rags story. The three guys achieve instant stardom on the "Tonight Show"; and the Entertainment Machine proceeds to grind them up and process them to make them commercial. Of course, the essence of what *made* them "commercial" is processed out, and their magic is gone. "Riotous!...bursting with daring ideas about how to do musicals. It transforms stand-up comedy into new unexpected forms of theatrical energy."—N.Y. Times. "Breezy, funny, vulgar, fresh, athletic, corny, sentimental and irresistible. The entire conception is strikingly original and oh those three guys! Should run as long as there's a laugh in us."—N.Y. Daily News. (Music available on rental.)

(#22688)

ROMANCE/ROMANCE
(LITTLE THEATRE—MUSICAL)
Book and lyrics by BARRY HARMAN
Music by KEITH HERRMANN

2 men, 2 women—2 Sets

Rejoice! Rejoice! Broadway has given us a brand-spanking-new, unabashedly romantic American musical comedy; actually, *two* of 'em, for this hit Broadway show is two musicals in one. Act I, "The Little Comedy", is based on Schnitzler's turn-of-the-century tale about a pair of Viennese worldlings who disguise themselves for an amatory adventure and then run into unforeseen complications—they actually start to *care* for each other! Act II, based on a Jules Renard play, is entitled "Summer Share". Set in Long Island's chic getaway spot The Hamptons, it concerns two married couples, enjoying summer refuge from the hustle and hassle of NYC. "Hurrah, hurrah for *Romance/Romance*."—Christian Science Monitor. "The evening sparkles with charm and intelligence." —N.Y. Times. "Barry Harman's lyrics are smart, Herrmann's music is bubbly and ardent."—N.Y. Daily News. "A double-dollop of the romantic spirit."—N.Y. Post. "A savvy little romp with a hip sensibility. Sweet, fresh and welcome."—Newsday. "A sweetheart of a musical that knows more about entertaining an audience than most of its larger, more pretentious peers."—Hearst Newspapers. (Music available on rental.) **Posters**. Restricted.

(#20108)